'**Don't start minding my feelings now. If you're trying to say I'm not sexy, go ahead,**' she invited. '**It's not exactly news to me.**'

There was a gleam in Theo's eyes that Beth found most disturbing as his glance slid down the length of her body before returning to her face.

'Now, that,' he approved, 'is a good look for you. Just carry on thinking what you are now and we're halfway there.'

'I'm thinking you are a hateful creep!'

The mocking glint in his dark eyes deepened. 'Why, Elizabeth, you're fighting it, but I think you're starting to like me.'

Kim Lawrence lives on a farm in rural Anglesey. She runs two miles daily, and finds this an excellent opportunity to unwind and seek inspiration for her writing! It also helps her keep up with her husband, two active sons, and the various stray animals which have adopted them. Always a fanatical consumer of fiction, she is now equally enthusiastic about writing. She loves a happy ending!

UNWORLDLY
SECRETARY,
UNTAMED GREEK

BY
KIM LAWRENCE

MILLS & BOON

First published in Great Britain 2010
Harlequin Mills & Boon Limited,
Eton House, 18-24 Paradise Road, Richmond, Surrey TW9 1SR

© Kim Lawrence 2010

ISBN: 978 0 263 87834 9

Harlequin Mills & Boon policy is to use papers that are natural, renewable and recyclable products and made from wood grown in sustainable forests. The logging and manufacturing process conform to the legal environmental regulations of the country of origin.

Printed and bound in Spain
by Litografia Rosés, S.A., Barcelona

UNWORLDLY
SECRETARY,
UNTAMED GREEK

CHAPTER ONE

THEO did not break stride as he walked across the room, but the expression on his dark lean features bore signs of lingering disbelief. Was he imagining it or had he just received a reprimand from his brother's mousey little secretary?

Extraordinary!

He replayed the scene in his head. When she'd deigned to glance up from her computer screen it had only been to dish up a look of supreme contempt before she'd politely explained that he was expected—adding, primly, *half an hour ago.*

He almost laughed but amusement rapidly tipped over into annoyance. The woman who ran his brother's professional life had irritated him from day one; there was just something about her. He couldn't pin it down—it wasn't *just* her prim pedantic manner, though that did grate on him, or even her overprotective attitude towards his brother.

Theo did not require the love or approval of those on his payroll, but he couldn't help but wonder when and how he had ever given her reason to view him as a dark force of evil.

She might privately have cast him as a villain in her own private melodrama—the woman did have a definite repressed Victorian thing going on—but up until today she had always been scrupulously polite in their dealings, even while projecting a level of hostility that was, quite frankly, bizarre.

He didn't know what her problem was, and he didn't want to know. He was prepared to cut her some slack because she was competent—actually, competence was the one thing she had in her favour. The same could not be said of many of her predecessors. Andreas's weakness for a pretty face meant that aptitude and ability frequently came at the bottom of his list of requirements during the interview process.

But Elizabeth Farley's ability not to go into meltdown when organising his brother's diary or the fact that she did not need to leave midway through a working morning to have her nails done didn't change the fact that she would not have been Theo's own first choice or even his last. But then, unlike his brother, he did not enjoy being the object of slavish adoration.

A flicker of distaste crossed his face as he considered the spaniel-like devotion and dedication she displayed that went way beyond the call of duty, but not, he suspected, as far as she would like it to go, not that anything was ever going to happen unless she ditched the ugly suits, grey in winter, taupe in summer.

His brother had no problem with slavish adoration but the women in Andreas's life could all have stepped from the pages of a fashion magazine—several had.

Female fashion was not a subject that was high on Theo's agenda of interesting topics but he appreciated confident women who made the effort to look good. The only effort Elizabeth Farley appeared to make was to hide any sign of her femininity.

The woman clearly had major issues but they were none of his concern. Being treated with an appropriate degree of respect in the workplace was, however, and while Theo did not expect grovelling sycophancy from employees within the building that bore his family name, he did *not* expect to be admonished by junior members of staff when he visited.

He had rarely—actually, never—been called upon to remind anyone who was boss, but he decided that this young woman needed to have her bubble of self-importance pricked.

When he stopped a few feet short of his brother's office door it was Theo's intention to do just that.

He turned and, slipping a button in his immaculately tailored jacket, cleared his throat. The small figure hunched behind the desk lifted her head and Theo's expression froze in icy put-down mode; behind the hideously unattractive spectacles she wore when doing paperwork, Elizabeth Farley's eyes were swimming with unshed tears.

Theo knew that some men were melted by female tears; he found such displays, even when they were not faked, irritating. So it was with some surprise that he found himself impelled to offer sympathy.

After a pause, he did so with a stilted reluctance. 'You are having a bad day?'

It wasn't just the understanding; it was the source, the suggestion of gentleness in a voice that she had previously only heard sounding hard, callous or sarcastic that loosed the sob locked in Beth's throat and she was utterly horrified to hear it emerge as something midway between a wail and a whimper.

It was so typical of the wretched man that he'd decided to be nice at totally the wrong moment; why couldn't he be his usual supercilious superior self?

Struggling to regain control and repeating *I will not cry* over and over in her head, she blinked furiously and mumbled something incoherent about allergies as she fought to escape the uncomfortably mesmeric eyes that held her own.

There were beads of sweat along her full upper lip when she did manage to tear her gaze clear.

It was utterly bizarre but, from the very first time she had seen him, Theo Kyriakis's eyes—deep set and fringed by long, lustrous curling lashes so dark they were almost black and shot with silver flecks—had bothered her. Actually, the rest of him made her pretty uneasy too.

Beth had always tried hard not to judge people on first impressions, but in the case of both Kyriakis brothers she had been unable to follow this rule.

Her gut reaction to both men had been instant and powerful. Beth didn't *dislike* many people but Theo Kyriakis wasn't *people*; he was the most coldly arrogant, condescending man she had ever met.

He was, in fact, the exact opposite of his brother; the moment Andreas had smiled at her, she had been his willing slave. The memory of that occasion brought a fresh flood of tears to her eyes.

Horrified by this unprofessional display, Beth bit her quivering lip and reached for a tissue from her bag, conscious all the time of the tall disapproving presence of the man everyone knew—no matter what it said in the firm's last upbeat Christmas letter—was the *only* boss of Kyriakis Inc looming over her.

Though it could not, she reflected dourly, be the first time he had reduced anyone to tears in the workplace. He did not exactly *ooze* empathy. As for tolerance! If she had been able, Beth would have laughed at the idea; Theo Kyriakis had *definitely* not been at the head of the queue when they'd handed out that one, though on other occasions he had obviously been first in line!

She blew her nose loudly and risked a surreptitious look

up at his bronzed patrician profile through her damp lashes. Even *she* had to admit, in her more objective moments, that Theo Kyriakis was not most people's idea of unhandsome and the overt in-your-face bold sexuality that he exuded, no matter what the occasion, it seemed to her, had probably never done him much harm.

It wasn't just that people looked at him and thought *gorgeous and sexy*—not intrinsically bad in itself and you couldn't blame a man for genetics—it was the fact that he obviously didn't give a damn *what* people thought about him that *really* got under her skin. The man's assurance and self-confident poise was utterly impregnable.

He walked into a room and conversations stopped, heads turned and eyes followed him, and it wasn't the immaculate tailoring and stunning good looks they stared at; the man literally oozed animal magnetism from every perfect pore.

Perfection was the problem. Theo Kyriakis put the cool into cool. The wretched man never had a hair out of place. Raised by a grandmother who valued such things, Beth, who had not been a naturally tidy child and still struggled to present a neat appearance, doubted that *neat* was an adjective that sprang to most people's minds as they followed his effortlessly elegant progression across a room.

It might make her strange but, to Beth's way of thinking, a man needed a few flaws, if only to make him halfway human! And he didn't have any. A take-me-or-leave-me attitude, she reflected with a resentful sniff, was easy when you knew people would always take you!

The underlying vulnerability she sensed in his brother was one of the things that had first attracted her to Andreas— well, maybe second after his extremely cute smile. The thing Andreas had that his brother lacked was *empathy*.

If *he* had found her crying, Andreas would have hugged

her, then made a teasing remark to make her laugh. He would not have stared at her with those spooky penetrating eyes. The thought of Theo Kyriakis hugging her should have been funny, but it wasn't. The idea of those muscular arms closing around her, drawing her against a body that was as hard as his eyes were cold made Beth's stomach muscles quiver with utter horror. Yes, that was definitely horror that she was feeling; what else could it be?

Looking down at the top of her glossy head, Theo winced as she blew her pink-tipped nose again—loudly. For a small nose, it made a lot of noise.

'Go home; I'll clear it with Andreas.' His offer, he told himself, was motivated by practicality, not kindness. It was not good business practice to have clients greeted by a hysterical female.

The casual offer brought Beth's head up, though her thoughts were still actively involved in creating a scene where she was locked in Theo Kyriakis's embrace—less fantasy and more waking nightmare.

'I couldn't possibly!' she protested, annoyed by the suggestion, she didn't work for him, but that didn't stop him flinging around his orders.

Her glance slid with dislike across his lean autocratic features; he never let anyone forget he was in charge for a second. Watching him undermine Andreas's authority, Beth had been forced to bite her tongue on more than one occasion but Andreas never complained. He was just too easy-going and nice-natured to complain.

Knowing how much Andreas hated making waves and enemies—his brother was a walking six feet five tidal wave—Beth frequently complained on his behalf, giving her a certain reputation for being what the polite within the building termed *overzealous* and the less polite called *hostile and scary*.

Scary did not earn her many friends, but it did grant her a certain amount of grudging respect; grudging respect and unrequited love meant her Friday nights were generally not wild affairs.

Theo's sable brows lifted at the vehemence of her response; he felt his attitude shift rapidly from mild sympathy to irritation.

'It's never good to bring personal problems to work.'

If he could maintain this discipline, even on the occasion some years earlier when his engagement had been broken off and his supposed broken heart had been the red-hot topic in numerous websites and his photo had been plastered over the covers of numerous trashy papers and magazines—not the best time in his life—it did not seem unreasonable to him to expect similar restraint from those in his employ.

The icy reproach made her eyes fly wide in indignation. 'I don't have a personal life!'

Theo arched a sardonic brow and watched the hot colour wash over her fair skin.

'You amaze me,' he murmured. It also amazed him that he was actually prolonging this conversation, but seeing someone as uptight as his brother's colourless robot secretary show her claws had a strange fascination—but then so did a car wreck for someone with nothing better to do—and he did.

Beth, her eyes glowing with dislike behind the lenses of her slightly misted spectacles, glared at him. Sarcastic rat!

'I have a great deal of work to do.'

'Few of us are indispensable, Miss Farley.'

Coded warning, threat…?

For once, Beth knew she would not be going to sleep trying to decipher the dark hidden meaning in one of Theo Kyriakis's sardonic throwaway comments, which might all be perfectly innocent, though it was hard to tell when he had a dark chocolate, deep accented voice that could make a shopping list sound deliciously sinister and lingered weirdly in your head for hours after a conversation.

Well, no more! In a year's time she would have forgotten what he sounded like. Yes, upbeat was good.

Yes, and being unemployed was *really* upbeat, especially with her overdraft situation!

Cutting off the inner dialogue abruptly, Beth lifted her chin. As an ex-employee, she no longer had to pander to this man's enormous ego, unlike the rest of the world!

'You can't sack me because I quit.'

Theo's brows rose as he looked from the handwritten envelope being held in a shaking hand towards him to the angry antagonistic eyes sparking green levelled at his face.

'Sack you?' he wondered, shaking his head in a mysti-fied manner. 'Did I miss something?'

Aware that she might have overreacted slightly, Beth's eyes fell from his. 'You said I wasn't indispensable,' she reminded him with a cranky sniff.

'And you think you are?'

'Of course not.'

Ignoring the interruption, he spoke across her. 'So you keep a resignation letter to hand for just such a moment?'

'Of course not. I—'

He turned his head to scan the envelope. 'And the name on that envelope does not appear to be mine. You do recall that you do not work for me?'

Beth rolled her eyes.

On paper, Andreas might be the boss in this office and, while he did have a degree of autonomy, Beth had learnt early on that all the major policy decisions were made by Theo Kyriakis. He was Kyriakis Inc, and nobody who knew anything about the company's meteoric rise under his management could question that.

Where his brother was concerned, Andreas did not do confrontation; he always took the route of least resistance.

'If you wanted me sacked, I'd be sacked.'

Theo tipped his head in acknowledgement of the challenging comment and drawled, 'What, and miss the possibility of future delightful discussions?' He stopped; he could actually hear her teeth grate. 'Look, I have no idea what has happened to upset you.'

And Theo had actually no idea why he was concerning himself with the question, beyond the fact that the efficiency of this office had a knock-on effect within the company.

And the smooth-running of Kyriakis Inc was always his concern.

'*You* happened!' Beth felt a twinge of guilt. No wonder he looked astonished by the comment; he hadn't actually done anything to earn her indignation—on this occasion.

Also she was guessing that he had limited experience of people, especially lowly secretaries like her, yelling at him.

She wasn't totally sure why she had made him the target of all her pent-up anger and frustration; the only thing he had done was notice she was miserable—he was the only person to notice.

It was Beth's turn to look astonished when, after a long pause, instead of blasting back with one of his legendary icy put-downs, he simply suggested, 'It might be an idea if you slept on this decision.'

Had his brother slept with her? Theo's expression froze and he didn't breathe for a full thirty seconds.

This rather startling explanation for the tears and tantrums fitted. How many times had he told Andreas that mixing romance and the workplace was the perfect recipe for disaster?

An expletive was an expletive in any language and Beth, who had never seen anything make a dint in this ultra-controlled man's composure, dropped her jaw as Theo swore, twitched the letter from her fingers and, after ripping it in half, tossed it in a waste paper basket.

'While you are not *indispensable*—' His sardonic smile flashed, the muscles in his jaw relaxing as he realised there was no way that Andreas would sleep with a woman who did not wear lipstick.

And Elizabeth Farley did not.

As Theo studied the surprisingly lush outline of her generous lips, he decided this was not a bad thing. Had she decided to highlight this particular natural asset, she might have proved a distraction for his easily distracted sibling, who might even have started wondering—this would have been a natural direction for any man's thoughts to take— what other assets she might be hiding beneath her buttoned collars and frumpy A-line skirts.

'—I think you are good at what you do,' he observed, continuing to study her lips.

For the second time in minutes Beth was stunned into silence; she had not imagined he had noticed her any more than he noticed the office furniture and now he was expressing a grudging appreciation—or was he?

She still wasn't sure.

Reluctantly, she met his eyes. *'You do?'*

'Am I wrong?'

Normally self-deprecating, Beth responded to the challenge glittering in his dark, heavy-lidded stare. 'I am good at what I do.'

So good that, from what he had observed, this office would fall apart without her in it. What, he wondered with a fresh surge of irritation, had Andreas done or not done to bring this about?

Taking sex out of the equation, as he now felt sure he safely could, he wasn't sure what was left.

A deep furrow formed between his brows as a possible answer occurred to him. 'Have *you* had a better offer?'

Beth's confused gaze lifted from the waste paper bin containing the remains of the letter she had redrafted three times already; fortunately, all she had to do was print out another. 'Offer?'

'Do not be coy,' he advised, a shade of impatience creeping into his abrupt manner. 'Has someone approached you?'

'For a *job*, you mean?' Her eyes widened at the startling suggestion. Did he really think she'd been headhunted?

He angled a questioning brow and Beth shook her head. 'No, I haven't.'

His eyes narrowed speculatively as his dark glance swept across her face. 'If challenge is a problem?' She was obviously intelligent, though the blank way she was looking at him at the moment suggested otherwise. 'If you are not feeling stretched with the work here?'

Theo, who thrived on challenge himself, understood this frustration of boredom and recognised it in others. Many people enjoyed being in a job that they could do on autopilot, but it was possible this woman was not one of those.

'Do you not think it more sensible to discuss the situation with Andreas before you make any rash decisions?'

The casual way he tossed the suggestion brought a mutinous sparkle to Beth's eyes as she got to her feet, her chest heaving with indignation.

Did the man actually think she had made this decision without a great deal of soul-searching? She was in no position to walk away from any job, let alone one this well paid but the alternative was even less palatable.

It was one thing to fall for the boss; it was another entirely to find yourself expected to help him pick the engagement ring for his girlfriend. After finding herself in that situation the previous week, Beth knew that she did not have the masochistic leaning required for this situation, or this job, any longer.

It probably made her weak, stupid or both but it wasn't as if she hadn't tried to fall out of love with him!

'I can't do it!' she yelled. 'If I have to watch him—'

Encountering the expression of total amazement etched on Theo Kyriakis's lean face, she dropped back into her chair and felt a mortified flush climb to her cheeks. 'You'd better go in,' she mumbled, allowing her hair to fall in a concealing curtain around her face.

Conscious of his silent presence, it felt like an age to Beth before he responded. The breath left her body in a sigh of relief as she heard the interconnecting door open.

Theo's thoughts still very much occupied by the baffling behaviour of Elizabeth Farley, the unexpected passion in her outburst and the sexiness of her quivering lips, it took him a few seconds to fully assimilate the scene he walked into.

His brother in a passionate clinch with the woman he had once been engaged to.

It was a moment of déjà vu—but not quite. On the previous occasion he had walked in on her in another man's arms, he had not been the intended target audience; it did not seem a big leap to assume that this time he was!

The scene was strikingly similar but there were significant differences—in both the scene and his reaction to it.

Last time had involved naked flesh but, happily, his

brother and Ariana were both fully dressed. Last time, his illusions had been shattered. He no longer had illusions, romantic or otherwise, which meant he could view the scene with an objectivity—tinged, admittedly, by distaste—he had not been capable of six years ago.

Six years ago, he'd been romantic and optimistic enough to consider himself the luckiest man in the world; he had met his soulmate—back then, he had firmly believed that such things existed—he had been *in love*.

And it had not been unpleasant to be the object of his friends' envy—he had a beautiful bride-to-be.

She was still beautiful and his brother clearly thought so too.

Was it genetic or was making a total fool of yourself with this woman a rite of passage that all Kyriakis men had to experience? If this was indeed so, it was a rite of passage that he had personally passed with flying colours! But no experience, however humiliating, was wasted and he had learnt from it.

In his professional life Theo had always worked on the premise that everyone had an angle, an agenda; now, thanks to Ariana, he had extended this attitude very successfully to his personal life.

He continued to enjoy sex—it was, after all, as much of a basic need as eating—but he no longer expected or wanted any mystical connection. He sometimes wondered how long he would have gone on believing the romantic fantasy he had bought into had not fate in the guise of a cancelled flight stepped in—the same fate that had brought him to the open door of his fiancée's apartment at the same moment as her much older ex-husband, Carl Franks.

Theo did not anticipate the time would ever come but if, by some cruel twist of fate, or possibly a blow to the head, he ever found himself in a situation where he was tempted to express his carnal appetite with the word *love* or *forever* Theo knew that replaying the deeply unpleasant scene etched into his brain would restore him to sanity.

On that previous occasion Theo had turned on his heel and walked away; that, unfortunately, was not on this occasion an option.

Now, his responsibility was clearly to save his brother.

It seemed unlikely that Andreas would appreciate his efforts. Though, on the plus side, Andreas, for all his faults, had never been what anyone would call a romantic and he had never displayed his own embarrassing youthful tendency to put women on pedestals; to recall the idealism of his youth still made Theo wince.

He wondered briefly whether Ariana had been unable to resist the temptation of his brother when an opportunity had presented itself or if she had gone out of her way to entrap Andreas, not that it mattered. He was genuinely astounded that she thought he would sit back and let this happen; maybe, in retrospect, it had sent the wrong message when he had permitted her to enjoy her petty revenge six years ago.

At the time he had calculated that responding to the interview she gave to a women's magazine would have only prolonged the public interest, even though the story she had shared with the readers had been fiction from start to finish.

I was crazy about Theo but I was shocked when he gave me an ultimatum. Theo made me choose between him and my career. He's very Greek; he wanted an old-fashioned sort of wife who would live her life through him.

She had phoned him to tell him that the article had been

directly responsible for getting her the contract as the face a new perfume ahead of the model who had been tipped for the job.

'*So thanks, Theo,*' she'd said, warning, '*but you still owe me.*'

Presumably this was payback time.

'Am I interrupting?'

The ironic question caused the couple, who were in a tight embrace, to pull apart. The woman rather ostentatiously adjusted the low gaping neckline of her dress and the man, looking flushed and embarrassed, dragged a hand through his tousled hair and cleared his throat.

'Theo…I…we…didn't hear you. We were…'

Theo arched a questioning brow at his clearly embarrassed brother and smiled. Actually, he wanted to throttle him; how could he *not* know that Ariana was poison, that she was motivated by two things—revenge and greed?

Like you did?

Ariana lifted a beautifully manicured hand to Andreas's lips and gave a complacent smile as she observed, in a voice that had been likened by more than one smitten man to a purr, 'Darling, Theo knows what we were doing.'

Andreas kept a wary eye on his brother as she pressed a lingering kiss to his lips. 'Well, I don't need to introduce you two, do I…?' he said, grinning weakly at his own joke.

Tall and universally considered good-looking, Andreas Kyriakis had learnt early in life that the warmth and charm of his smile would tip the balance of most situations in his favour, but on this occasion his smile was wary as he reached for the chilled champagne.

The unease vanished as his attention turned to his

beautiful bride-to-be. As he popped the cork he was unable
to stifle a smile of triumph.

It was his brother's turn to be second best.

Ariana had not wanted Theo but she wanted him.

CHAPTER TWO

'THAT was all a very long time ago. We were children, weren't we, Theo?' Ariana took the glass of champagne and looked at the older brother through the mesh of her darkened lashes, experiencing a moment's uncertainty as she realised that Theo was looking relaxed when he was meant to be denouncing her to Andreas and flinging ultimatums.

'Infants,' Theo agreed as his sardonic glance brushed the rock sparkling on Ariana's finger. 'At least I was.'

As he smiled and watched the puzzled pout settle on Ariana's lips he found himself comparing the cosmetically enhanced fullness, which he found not even vaguely inviting, with the softer and much sexier lushness of Elizabeth Farley's naturally pink lips.

Well, now he had the cause of the tears and tantrums in the outer office; it appeared he wasn't the only one unhappy about that diamond.

'You should have been at Ariana's birthday bash in Paris, Andreas,' he commented offhandedly.

He paused, a flicker of something close to shock moving across the reflective surface of his dark eyes—he had just thought *sexy, inviting* and *Elizabeth Farley* in the same sentence!

How had that happened?

'But, no, I remember now, you were doing your exams. What was it, Ariana—your thirtieth?' he asked innocently.

Ariana's careful smile slipped; her blue eyes were hard as she corrected sharply, 'I was still in my twenties.'

'Yes, that would be right,' Theo agreed, feeling no remorse for attacking one of Ariana's weak spots. 'I did have a thing for older women at that age. Do you remember there were balloons and clowns?'

'There was a famous mime artist,' Ariana told Andreas, 'and Theo fell asleep.'

'Age isn't relevant when you're in love,' Andreas said quickly and with enough defensiveness in his manner to reveal this was not an opinion he had formed in the moment. 'And Theo was never a child; he emerged with a phone in one hand and a contract in the other.'

Theo accepted the glass from his brother and turned to close the door behind him while he fought to control his temper.

He would lock his brother in a cellar if that was what it took, but he was hoping to come up with a more imaginative solution.

Failure was not something that Theo considered.

Considering failure was not the attitude that had quadrupled the profits of the already prominent international company he'd become head of after his father's death; considering failure was not why Theo was spoken of as one the most influential figures of the decade, the template for any man who wanted to make his first billion before he was thirty.

'So what is the occasion?' he drawled, his dark glance sliding once more to the ostentatious diamond before his eyes lifted and he looked directly at his brother. 'Or is that a foolish question?' he asked, resisting the strong impulse to yell, *Have you lost your tiny mind?* And added, 'I take it congratulations are in order.'

Ariana fluttered her lashes and waved her left hand at him. 'We wanted you to be the first to know, Theo.'

But he wasn't; the girl who was probably composing a second resignation letter as they spoke had known.

'I'm touched,' Theo said, his thoughts turning to the problem at hand—namely, how to make his brother see that he would be better off marrying a barracuda, or at least safer.

Forcibly beating the information into his brother's head was an appealing option and it would have the added bonus of making Theo feel moderately better in the short term but, as this was the reaction Ariana was probably hoping for, he was not going to give her the opportunity to call him the jealous brother.

It was actually not jealousy but nausea he felt as he watched Andreas slide his arm around Ariana's slender waist.

His brother's expression was tinged with defiance as he hugged her to him and announced with pride, 'Ariana has agreed to be my wife. I hope…we hope that this won't be awkward…'

There was only a moment's pause before Theo lifted his glass and drawled, 'Not awkward for me. Congratulations.'

Andreas, his relief visible, relaxed and reached for another glass. 'I'll just take one out for Beth; she should join us.'

Theo held out a hand. 'I'll do it.'

Before his brother could respond to his offer, Ariana intervened. 'Beth?' the blonde echoed. She adopted an expression of wide-eyed bewilderment as she asked, 'Who's Beth?'

'Beth—my secretary, Beth—you passed her on the way in; you've seen her every time you've been here, darling.'

'Oh, her!'

Theo watched as the glamorous model dismissed the younger woman with a laugh and went on to convince his brother that to invite his assistant, who was obviously a shy little creature, to join in with what was, after all, a family occasion would only embarrass her.

Andreas gave a shrug. 'I suppose you're right; this is a family thing.'

Despite his agreement, it was obvious to Theo that his brother was not happy to exclude his assistant.

Now this was interesting. It did not surprise him that Ariana had picked up on the fact that the girl was desperately in love with her boss; she was about as subtle as a slap in the face—she looked at Andreas as if she was on a carb-free diet and he was freshly baked bread.

But Ariana's determination to exclude her did.

Did she actually view the younger girl as a threat, a possible rival for Andreas's affections that had to be kept out of the picture?

His eyes narrowed slightly as he summoned a mental picture of the features of the woman who had not seemed a *shy creature* when she had yelled at him moments earlier.

Possibly it was the novelty value of her attitude towards him that made it surprisingly easy for Theo to recall her small heart-shaped face, big eyes and, of course, her soft mouth in such detail.

He still didn't think it was possible that anything had happened between his brother and Elizabeth Farley but if Ariana was insecure about the girl, who could make a nun look flamboyant by comparison, if she considered her a threat, what had or hadn't happened was not the point.

The point was, he might be able to use Ariana's obvious

insecurities to his advantage… As he listened to his brother describing their plans for the wedding, the bones of a plan began to formulate in his head.

Beth tried to turn a deaf ear to the sounds emanating from the adjoining room. She was doing quite well until she started at the loud distinctive sound of a champagne cork popping and deleted the page of statistics that had taken her the entire morning to meticulously research.

'Get a grip, Beth!' she growled with a grimace of self-disgust as some of the moisture pooling in her hazel eyes escaped.

Biting her wobbling lower lip, she angrily blotted a tear from her cheek with the back of her hand.

'What did you expect, you idiot—that he'd stay single? That he'd wait for you? That was *really* going to happen!'

It would not be so bad, Beth told herself as she blotted her face and went about retrieving the deleted figures, if it hadn't been *that* woman.

Obviously, no woman was good enough for Andreas, who possessed the rare qualities that made him perfect husband material, but there was *not good enough* and then there was *Ariana*.

An image of the willowy blonde's suspiciously smooth face flashed before her eyes and she scowled. There was just something about Ariana Demetrios that really got under her skin—correction, it was *everything*, from the older woman's fake smile to her fake breasts.

The bitchy thought afforded her a brief moment of satisfaction before the self-pity crowded in once more.

If it had been anyone else he had fallen for, she could have been happy for him… Well, not happy, but resigned at least.

She didn't feel resigned; she felt…Beth pressed a hand

to her stomach and shifted restlessly in her swivel chair…
actually, she felt sick. Her dreams had just died and a person
needed dreams, or at least she did, even of the impossible
variety.

And while sitting by and watching Andreas work his way
through every drop dead gorgeous blonde with a D cup in
the City had not been pleasant, it had at least left her room
to hope.

Now, she didn't have that—he was getting married, and
to the toxic Ariana!

At least she had her pride intact. Andreas had no idea
that she had been smitten from that very first smile; Beth
comforted herself with this crumb. If she had had a scrap
of sense, of course, she reflected miserably, she would have
walked back out through the door that first day, but better
late than never, she decided, patting the reprinted letter that
lay safe in her pocket.

It might not seem like it now but Andreas had done her
a favour—it was about time she got a real life, even a real
boyfriend, she told herself, struggling to work up much
enthusiasm for the idea.

She had to start thinking about the future as a place full
of exciting possibilities and step one was handing in her
notice. Another job might even leave her time for that night
class in business studies she had wanted to do for ages.

'Be positive, Beth,' she told herself as she made a fresh
attempt to retrieve the information that Andreas had asked
her to have on his desk by Friday.

Despite her best intentions, she lifted her head, a wistful expression forming on her soft features as she heard
the familiar warm tones of her boss's voice; she heard him
laugh, a warm sound, then heard the deeper, more vibrant
tone of his brother.

Her expression hardened as an image of Theo Kyriakis

flashed into her head. It always amazed her that the brothers, separated by only five years, could be so dissimilar. How could their shared gene pool produce two men who were opposites in every way imaginable?

The only thing they did share, apparently, was a weakness for one particular blonde model.

When Andreas had been spotted leaving the building with Ariana the day before, the place had started buzzing with speculation. Everyone had wanted to know—were they an item, was Andreas dating the woman who had dumped his elder brother so publicly?

When asked, Beth had diplomatically pretended ignorance but, like everyone else, she had wondered how a man with Theo's ego would react to such a situation. Though, unlike the majority of people she spoke to, she understood totally why Ariana, or any woman, would prefer Andreas to his elder brother.

Her expression softened as she thought of Andreas. Why did people constantly have to compare him to his autocratic brother? It was so unfair. Andreas was a good-looking man by any standards. Athletic, six-foot, he had regular features, warm brown eyes, wavy brown hair and a gorgeous smile. Taken feature for feature, he was actually far more conventionally good-looking than his elder brother but even Beth, who didn't like the man, had to admit that it was Theo Kyriakis who commanded attention and lustful female glances when the two brothers entered a room together.

People did not notice the slight irregularity of his features; they were too busy noticing his startling eyes, carved cheekbones, bronzed skin and the almost indecent sensuality of his wide mobile mouth.

Of course the man had the advantage of several inches on his brother, six five with broad shoulders, long legs and a sleek athletic body. He was an extraordinarily attractive man if you went for the dark, brooding type, which she didn't.

The sound of female laughter drove the lingering image of Theo Kyriakis's dark features from her head. She clenched her teeth. Ariana might be beautiful but her laugh was borderline shrill—not that Andreas appeared to mind, but then men were in general willing to overlook such details when they were dazzled by pouty lips, long blonde hair and a body that made even the most outrageous style look fantastic.

Get a grip, Beth.

'See you at eight, Theo?' Beth heard Andreas say as the door opened. She tensed and trained her eyes on the blank computer screen.

She glanced up in time to see Andreas place a possessive arm around his fiancée's slim waist as he steered her towards the door. 'The entire family will be there.'

'With such a treat in store, how can I resist?'

The dry response drew a good-natured chuckle from his brother. 'Bring someone, if you like.'

His brother bowed his head in ironic acknowledgement of the generous offer and watched, his expression unreadable, as his younger brother turned briefly to the young woman seated silently at the big desk beside the door.

'I can leave the paperwork on the Crane contract to you, can't I, Beth, sweetheart? And those figures—you will have them ready for the morning?' Without waiting for a reply, he added, 'They really need the paperwork from this morning's meeting by close of play today. You're an angel. I don't know what I'd do without you.'

Beth looked up, feeling an uncharacteristic surge of resentment and thought, *Well, you'll soon find out*.

'So eight, Theo?'

Beth wondered if Theo Kyriakis had heard the note of

challenge and almost instantly felt foolish. Theo Kyriakis was not a man who missed anything, unless it was a secretary, not that she'd minded that he acted as if she were invisible—until today.

Actually, today had made her realise that she preferred it that way.

Beth watched through her lashes as Theo Kyriakis inclined his closely cropped dark head, whether in acknowledgement of the challenge or the invitation she couldn't tell, but then her boss's elder brother was not a man who gave a lot away.

'I'll be there.'

The couple left the office, leaving the echo of their laughing voices and the heavy scent of the fragrance that the future Mrs Kyriakis favoured.

Did the perfume evoke painful memories for Theo Kyriakis?

Anyone else and her tender heart would have ached but Beth felt no twinge of empathy at the possibility that Theo Kyriakis found it painful, maybe even heartbreaking, to see the woman he had once planned to marry wearing his brother's ring.

The man just didn't invite sympathy, she decided, studying his dark lean face. Perhaps he was hiding the pain; if so, he was doing pretty well!

Beth moved an already neat stack of files from one side of the desk to the other and waited for Theo Kyriakis to leave.

He didn't.

She risked a look up at him and was startled to discover that his heavy-lidded dark stare was trained directly on her own face.

Beth shifted uncomfortably in her seat and pushed her

glasses up her nose before venturing a faint vague smile in his general direction and returning her attention to her desk.

She started a little as he placed an untouched glass of champagne on her desk. 'There's more in the bottle if you'd like to join me to toast the happy couple?'

Beth would have found an invitation to jump into the Thames more alluring but she kept her manner polite. 'This is the middle of a working day for me, Mr Kyriakis, and I'm just the hired help,' she reminded him, addressing her response to the middle button of his beautifully tailored grey jacket.

'But you would like to be more than that?'

The unexpected question made her stiffen—actually, it was not a question; it was a statement.

Before she could respond to it, he said abruptly, 'Why do you dress that way?'

Her defensive glance swung upwards from his beautifully tailored designer suit to discover that he was studying her own grey flannel suit with an expression of fastidious distaste written on his lean face.

'What way?' Beth, who had three identical ones in her wardrobe and a selection of plain blouses to wear with them, asked.

Gran had always advised her to go for quality when selecting clothes and Beth followed her advice, though she stopped short at the matching gloves and handbag that Prudence Farley considered essential for a well turned out lady.

In the long-term, Gran had counseled, it was cheaper to choose quality rather than buy trendy junk and she was right, but the *junk* did look fun, Beth sometimes thought wistfully.

She lifted her chin defiantly as her hand went to her throat, where her cream blouse was buttoned up to the neck.

After three years of not noticing she existed, he was suddenly interested in her clothes?

'Is there something I can help you with, Mr Kyriakis?' Had he been drinking?

The scandal-hungry media had never suggested a weakness for drink, just for tall leggy blondes, but who knew, she thought, curiosity drawing her eyes to his face. The arrogant cast of his strong features did not suggest weakness or lack of control, if you discounted the sensual fullness of his upper lip.

Conscious of a sinking shivery sensation low in her stomach, Beth tore her strangely reluctant gaze from his mouth and found it wandering straight into the path of his dark eyes and she immediately dumped the drinking idea.

There was nothing blurry or unfocused about his manner. Drinking implied a human weakness and the elder Kyriakis brother didn't appear to tolerate those in himself or other people.

Theo doesn't tolerate fools gladly, Andreas was fond of observing. In her own mind, Beth translated this as code for the fact that he was impatient and intolerant.

'Quite possibly.'

Beth's polite smile grew wary as she watched his wide, sensually sculpted lips curve into a smile that did not reach his dark eyes; the speculative light in their obsidian depths was making her feel deeply uneasy.

'But of course you didn't mean that, did you? Do I make you feel uncomfortable?'

'No, of course not,' Beth lied. 'I didn't intend to be rude, but I have a lot of work to do.' She would be lucky, Beth reflected, to make it home before seven—actually, eight— she corrected, recalling the meeting she had scheduled with the manager at the nursing home.

The request to see her had worried Beth, especially as

the manager had been reluctant to elaborate further on the phone, but he had reassured her that there was no problem with her grandmother.

She had a horrid feeling that the news might involve a fresh hike in the fees.

The move to the nursing home had been Gran's idea; she had not even informed Beth that she had booked herself in until the arrangements were made. Beth had been horrified by the idea but her doubts had been soothed when Prudence Farley had said she only intended staying a few weeks.

That had been six months ago and Gran showed no inclination to move back home. The place, she confided to Beth, was like a five-star hotel. At home, she could go a week without seeing anyone but Beth and the vicar's wife; here, there was never a dull moment and she had made so many new friends.

Beth loved her new zest for life but she was worried; the place was not only run like a five-star hotel but they charged similar rates. Her gran remained cheerfully oblivious to the fact that her savings had run out in the first three months and, when the subject came up, Beth, concerned about worrying her grandmother, was deliberately vague.

It was a constant battle to meet the costs and keep the house going. Beth was only living in three rooms of the big sprawling Victorian mansion that her grandmother had come to as a new bride, but the upkeep was a financial drain that gave her nightmares.

She called it a nightmare; the bank manager called it her get out of jail card.

When she had pointed out that she wasn't in jail, he had said darkly, 'Not yet.'

Beth wasn't sure if he was joking or not but none of his dire predictions had made her change her mind. She was not selling up to a developer; the house would be there when Gran decided to come home.

The bank manager had been visibly frustrated by her intransigent attitude.

'Miss Farley, your attitude does you credit but it is hardly practical. Let me be blunt. Your grandmother is a very old lady; it seems unlikely she will ever come home. And these figures—' he sighed as he flicked through the papers laid out in front of him '—I'm afraid they suggest you cannot pay for your grandmother's care and eat.'

Beth, in an attempt to lighten the atmosphere, had joked, 'I need to lose weight.'

He had not seen the joke. 'I would suggest there is no choice. When your grandmother gave you Power of Attorney it was a situation like this that she had in mind.'

Beth had thanked him for his advice because she knew he meant well but she had remained adamant she would not sell up or contemplate the possibility of her gran not coming home.

She knew that Gran loved the place as much as she did. The sprawling Victorian house had, in estate agent speak, a wealth of original features but very little in the way of modern conveniences. Beth had lived there since her parents' death in a train crash when she was seven.

'You want me to leave so that you can weep in privacy?'

The casual question made her stiffen and brought her eyes back to his lean face. How did a man who had not given her the same degree of attention he afforded the office furniture on his visits come to know about the knot of misery lodged like a lead weight in her aching throat?

'I don't know what you mean...'

He cut her off with an impatient gesture. 'You're in love with my brother.'

CHAPTER THREE

BETH felt the blood drain from her face as she stared at him in horror. 'That's totally ridiculous!'

He raised his brows in mock surprise. 'I did not realise it was meant to be a secret. My apologies.'

It took a massive amount of willpower not to drop her gaze. Tired of pushing her glasses back up her nose, she took them off and placed them on the desk before fixing him with a glare of thinly disguised loathing.

'You know what you can do with your apologies and your sick sense of humour!'

The transformation was nothing short of incredible. She still wasn't a raving beauty but if his brother saw her with her cheeks flushed, her small bosom heaving and her eyes glittering with anger he would have noticed her.

'Andreas has just got engaged to a beautiful woman. You wish to wallow in self-pity and perhaps look at the photo you keep in your wallet.' The cynicism in his smile deepened as he watched her eyes fly to her handbag. 'No, it was a lucky guess—I have not been going through your bag.'

'Is that some sort of joke?' The joke, she realized, feeling sick, was herself. Did everyone know…? The idea of being the butt of gossip, maybe even *pity*, made her feel physically sick.

She gathered her dignity around her and lifted her chin, inadvertently winning Theo's admiration for her gutsy effort, and said coldly, 'I work for your brother. We do not have a personal relationship...unlike you and...' She broke off guiltily, her eyes widening in dismay.

She had never kicked anyone when they were down—not that he looked down—but, under his nasty cold exterior, Theo Kyriakis had to have his normal share of emotional vulnerability...Their eyes connected, his glittered with a combination of amused contempt and challenge that made her rapidly rethink her vulnerability theory as antagonism traced a path down her spine—all this man had was an overreaching ego and stone as dark and cold as his eyes where his heart should be!

'Unlike me and...?'

She shook her head and straightened a pile of already straight papers. 'I really am very busy.' She aimed her smile at some point over his left shoulder.

'You possibly refer to my relationship with the delightful Ariana...?' He arched a questioning brow.

The dratted man. Why wouldn't he just let it drop? Beth thought. 'That was a long time ago.' Had it been a lucky guess or was she really that obvious? And, if he had guessed, did that mean that Andreas knew as well?

A film of hot mortification washed over her pale skin at the thought. Hot, she slipped the top button of her blouse and then the second because her chest felt tight.

Theo felt his eyes drawn to the bare few inches of flesh at her throat; he could actually see the blue-veined pulse spot on her neck vibrating. 'The past is frequently relevant to the present.'

Having delivered this seemingly unrelated philosophical observation, he pulled a chair from the wall, dragged it to her desk and straddled it, placing his hands along the back of it before he returned his attention to Beth.

Beth, who no longer wanted an explanation for this conversation, lowered her gaze as far as his hands, curved lightly over the back of the designer chair. He actually had good hands—elegant but strong, with long tapering fingers—and sent up a silent prayer for him to leave.

She needed to think—not a possibility while he was enjoying his cat-and-mouse game with her—the man clearly got some twisted pleasure from seeing her squirm.

'I suspect that part of Ariana's attraction for my little brother is our previous relationship; he's very competitive.'

Beth's shaking hand knocked down the neat stack of files on the desk as her head came up with a jerk. '*He's* competitive!' She scanned the dark features of the man seated opposite with open incredulity. It obviously didn't even occur to him that she just preferred Andreas to him. My God, this man's ego was simply unbelievable.

After a slight pause Theo conceded her comment with an amused quirk of his lips, the action drawing Beth's attention to the overtly sensual curve. The shivery sensation in her tummy intensified.

'All right, *we*—it's a brother thing,' he revealed casually.

Beth dragged her oddly reluctant eyes from his mouth. Even when he had ignored her totally she had felt uncomfortable being in the same room as Theo Kyriakis; now he wasn't ignoring her, now he was having what in his twisted mind probably passed for a conversation the feeling had intensified to a point where all she wanted to do was run from the room.

Get a grip, Beth. 'It may be your thing but it's not Andreas's.'

Frustrated by her inability to place the shadow of an emotion that moved at the back of his eyes, Beth found herself unfavourably comparing his cold, sardonic temperament with Andreas's open, approachable, sunny character.

It was a struggle to believe they were even related. Andreas was a sunny day and this vile man was night, dark, impenetrable and full of hidden dangers.

'I bow to your superior knowledge of my brother.' He dipped his dark head towards her and continued in the same sarcastic manner that had a nail scraping on blackboard effect on Beth's nerve endings. 'You are clearly an expert on the subject.' Perhaps his brother had dropped a casual kiss on her cheek once and she had been fantasising about it ever since—or had they gone further?

Irritated by the returning theme, Theo rejected the idea before his mind supplied the accompanying images which, for some irrational reason, he found more disturbing than the very real image of his brother kissing his own ex-lover.

Elizabeth Farley might look a lot better minus the awful clothes but Andreas was not the type to look beyond the surface or even be curious.

Yet Ariana did have the insight he lacked. She clearly felt this pale, spiky girl was a potential threat so maybe his brother was attracted and didn't even realise it?

Beth gritted her teeth and felt the colour flame in her cheeks; she had never wanted to wipe the smug smirk off a blackboard!

'No...no, I didn't mean that I...you get to know someone when you work for them; we're close.' Her cheeks flamed at the belated realisation of the sordid interpretation this hateful man might put on this comment and she added quickly, 'Not obviously close like—'

He halted her mumbling, embarrassed retraction with a

languid motion of one hand. 'You think that my brother is above such petty things as sibling rivalry, you think he is noble and—'

His sarcasm brought a flush to her cheeks. 'I think he is in love.' Being selfless, she decided, was not all it was cracked up to be.

'And you think you know all about love?'

She stared at him, sitting there looking what nine out of ten women—and these odds were granting her own sex more sense than they probably had—would call perfect and she felt the leaden lump of misery that had lain in her throat all day melt as a wave of incandescent rage swept over her.

He didn't have a clue what it was like to be her! She jumped to her feet, sending her chair hurtling into the wall behind her. 'I know a damn sight more about it than you do!' she yelled, recoiling slightly as the volume of her own voice hit her.

He did not look offended by her accusation.

'So you accept the situation and walk away. Don't you want to fight for him?'

'And how do you suggest I do that?' Her response made him realise just how far past sensible she had allowed the conversation to go. 'Look, you might have nothing to do but I think this joke has gone far enough...' Silently willing him to take the hint, Beth thought her prayers had been answered when Theo rose to his feet.

Her relief was short-lived. He made no move to leave. Instead, he dragged a hand through his hair and allowed his gaze to travel from the soles of her sensible shoes to the top of her glossy head. 'One obvious suggestion springs to mind. You could dress like a woman and not like a middle-aged librarian.'

An angry flush of mortification mounted her cheeks. 'I'm not about to pretend I'm someone I'm not.'

'An admirable sentiment, but do you suppose that Ariana gets to look the way she does without a hell of a lot of effort? And I'm not talking about the Botox. Ever heard the comment *no pain, no gain?* Well, in Ariana's case it's *no food, no gain.*'

'She's naturally slim!' Beth protested.

He let out a deep growl of laughter. 'You really are naive.'

Beth clenched her teeth. 'If I was in love with your brother—which I am not—I'd be happy he has found someone to make him happy,' she retorted piously.

'Which makes you either incredibly virtuous and totally boring or a liar.' He watched a fresh wave of warm colour wash over her skin and realised that she wore no make-up at all, but then he conceded that a woman with skin that smooth and flawless did not need to. 'You do realise,' he drawled, 'that most men find the doormat mentality a real turn-off?'

Beth levelled a glare of seething dislike at his lean sardonic face. 'I don't claim to be selfless, though that would be preferable to being totally *selfish*,' she flung back, too angry to reconsider the wisdom of insulting this man.

He had a well earned reputation for being utterly ruthless, and she knew he would not lose any sleep about sacking a humble secretary. Andreas might try to prevent it, but she had seen him cave in under pressure from Theo far too often to have any illusions that he would stand up to his brother and save her.

He arched a brow and observed, with an amused look, 'The saint has claws.' And, now that he thought about it, Theo realized, rather spectacular eyes he was able to see properly now that she had removed the glasses.

On anyone else, he would have suspected that the colour—deep green shot with flecks of amber—of those almond-shaped eyes had been achieved with the assistance of contact lenses, but with this woman, who appeared to go out of her way to blend into the background, he seriously doubted it!

Finding herself the focus of the prolonged scrutiny of his heavy-lidded stare made her want to crawl out of her skin. Resisting the temptation to retreat behind the heavy curtain of hair that hung around her small face, she slid her fingers into the thick skein and tucked it behind her ears. Gran always said she had beautiful hair, but Beth would have happily exchanged her impossibly thick mop of mousey-brown wayward waves for smooth blonde or exciting red hair.

'He does not see you as a woman; he sees you as a piece of office furniture.'

Beth's breath caught as though someone had just landed a blow, which in a way they had; Theo used the truth with the ruthless surgical precision of a blade. Was he born this vicious? she wondered.

She opened her mouth to automatically refute his cruel assertion and then her innate honesty kicked in; he was probably right, she thought dully.

Theo hadn't finished. 'Do you think he even knows the colour of your eyes? You are useful to him; he knows that you will go the extra mile for him.' He stopped, satisfied he had made his point.

Make it any more clearly and she'd be stretched out in a dead faint at his feet; she was looking at him like a child who had just been told there was no Santa Claus.

Aware that he was breathing too hard, Theo made a conscious effort to slow his inhalations. It was a long time since he had allowed anyone to get under his skin enough to make him feel guilty about his actions in any way. And why should he feel guilty?

It was totally irrational. All he'd done was tell her the truth, though possibly, he conceded, he might have done so less brutally.

It was just the way she idolised Andreas which made him want to shake some sense into her head; the woman was wasting her life mooning like some heroine in a romantic novel over a man who did not know she was alive.

'You're right.'

The sudden admission drew his alert gaze to her face. She looked pale but composed as she elaborated, 'I am in love with Andreas and, yes, he doesn't know I'm alive, not in that way, but I'm leaving.' Her slender shoulders lifted in a shrug. 'So the problem goes away.'

The admission had clearly cost her. Theo felt a fresh stirring of admiration—whatever else she was, the woman had guts.

'Excellent—now we are on the same page.'

Beth sank back down into her chair, her wary gaze trained on his lean face. Once again, Theo had surprised her. She had fully expected he would be unable to resist the opportunity to rub her nose in it but, instead, he had allowed her admission to pass, almost without comment, and had turned all enigmatic.

She didn't want to ask but she couldn't help herself. 'What page would that be?' That they would share anything, even a page, seemed extremely unlikely to Beth.

'We each, for our own reasons, think it would be a mistake for Andreas to marry Ariana.' He dipped his head and waited for her response.

'That really has nothing to do…' The sardonic expression in his expressive eyes stopped her mid-sentence. 'All right,' she conceded crankily. 'I don't think that Ariana is good enough for Andreas.' Now, she thought, this was where he pointed out that she was hardly what anyone would call objective.

'She is poison.'

Beth was unable to display a similar restraint in her response. 'You didn't always think that.' She encountered his wry stare and blushed. 'Well, you were going to marry her yourself,' she added defensively. Everyone knew that name-calling was a classic response of the dumped lover.

'Any woman I find attractive is immediately of interest to Andreas. If we were lovers, he would find you irresistible.'

An image of his sleek, bronzed, powerful male body appeared in her head—an uneducated guess, but enough to send embarrassed colour flying to her cheeks. So it wasn't the first time she had wondered what he looked like naked, and where was the harm in that?

Her defiant gaze slid from his as she scoffed, 'And back to planet earth.' If offered the opportunity to find out for real, she would have run for the hills.

'Would it not be pleasant for you to have Andreas notice you are a woman?' His dark eyes skimmed her body, his glance disturbingly intimate as it lingered on the suggestion of curves.

Beth, her mind still spinning from the moments she had allowed herself to imagine him without his clothes, was thrown into total confusion at the thought that he might be doing the same about her.

'I...' Beth swallowed to alleviate the dryness in her throat. In her chest, her heart was pounding like a piston.

'I have a proposal. Are you willing to hear me out?'

Beth regarded him warily. 'Would it matter if I said no?'

Her ironic response drew a laugh. 'But you won't. We both have reasons for wanting this engagement to end.'

While he did not elaborate on his own reasons, it did not, Beth thought, take a genius to figure them out. Theo Kyriakis still carried a torch for his old love. Seeing her again had resurrected all those old feelings and he was determined that his brother would not have her.

Maybe equally determined that he would win her back.

Well, good luck to him. In Beth's mind, the pair were well suited; they deserved one another!

'If we pool out resources,' he continued, 'I think we might be able to pull it off.'

There was no *might* in his voice, just cast iron certainty, but that was Theo Kyriakis—a man who was pretty much a stranger to self-doubt. As for resources, Beth was using all hers just to stay upright.

'You will need suitable clothes, hair and so forth but yes...' he narrowed his eyes, as though visualising the changes he spoke of '...I think it will work.'

'Suitable for what?' It cost nothing to humour him and she was actually curious to know where he was going with this.

'The celebration meal tonight, we will go together as a couple and test the waters.'

She waited for the punchline but none came. Her jaw dropped. 'You're serious...my God, you're insane.'

Theo looked totally unperturbed by her response. 'One man's insanity is another man's inspiration.'

This smooth retort drew a choked laugh from Beth—he really was unbelievable.

'Inspired!' She shook her head. 'You're not inspired; you're stark raving mad! No one is going to believe we're a couple.'

'They will; just trust me on this, Elizabeth.' She looked at him, so smooth and persuasive, and thought sure, like she'd trust a politician during election year. 'When we were kids, Andreas always wanted the flavour of ice cream I got.'

'I'm not an ice cream.' As if she could become part of some romantic triangle! Or was it quadrangle? *Absurd* did not do the suggestion justice.

'But you are—or could be—an attractive woman.'

It was a clinical assessment and one that was made with no hint of sexual suggestion. Despite this, or maybe because of it, under her dismissive expression Beth experienced a swell of tentative excitement.

Could she really be beautiful?

She shook her head and adopted a scornful expression but, underneath, the tempting possibilities continued to slide through her mind. What would it be like to have Andreas look at her as though she were an attractive woman?

'What have you got to lose?'

'I'm assuming you're talking about something beyond sanity and self-respect?'

'You want Andreas.' The blunt pronouncement made Beth shift uncomfortably. 'Will you ever forgive yourself if you don't try?'

Theo watched the expressions flit across her face and gave a nod of satisfaction. He had sold enough deals to know when he had clinched it; she might not be happy about it and it might take a few more minutes of fairly pointless protest but Elizabeth Farley would play the game.

CHAPTER FOUR

'You need to make Andreas think of you as a woman.'

She regarded him with a cranky glare. 'So you said, but just what does he think I am now?'

'He thinks you're Angela Simmons.' He watched her struggle not to ask the obvious.

She lasted a minute or so before she sighed, 'All right, who is Angela Simmons?' It was not a name she was familiar with and Beth was pretty familiar with all the women Andreas had dated over the past three years.

'We both got sent away to an English prep school; she was the kid who wrote all his history essays until the staff caught on.'

His father had been more appalled to learn that the establishment three generations of Kyriakis males had studied at now allowed females to attend than he had been at his younger son's scheme to cheat the system.

He had been a lot more annoyed when the same school had three years earlier written *Theo dislikes authority and is not a team player* on his own report card.

It was a frequently occurring theme during his school days and it never failed to produce a furious response from his father, who worked hard to eradicate the rebellious streak in the son he considered too emotional and arty. Theo did not resent his father's attitude; he considered he had been tough but fair and he had only ever had Theo's best interests at heart. He considered it his job to prepare his son for the future that was mapped out for the eldest Kyriakis son.

His father's voice echoed in his mind. *Along with privilege, Theo, comes responsibility.*

When he had added, *You weren't born a leader, Theo, but we can make you one,* Theo had known he was thinking of his elder brother, Niki, who had died so tragically young.

Niki had been born a leader.

He had not embarrassed his father with emotional outbursts—he had been charming and universally admired. Niki had not spent his free time alone in the art room; he had captained the school sports teams to triumph.

Niki was dead and it was his fault. Nobody had ever come out and said so, but it was what they thought—it was what he thought.

He snapped back to the present to find Beth regarding him with mute dislike and continued, 'Andreas didn't pay her or bully her; she just wanted to do something nice for him because she worshipped him.'

'You're comparing me to a teenager?' A teenager had the excuse of extreme youth—she didn't.

'They were seven.'

'Seven? He was sent away to school at seven?' At seven, she had been climbing into her gran's bed every night after waking from night terrors.

'We both were.'

'That's barbaric!' she exclaimed.

Theo shrugged dismissively in response to her shocked response but, should he ever have a son—a possibility that seemed at present doubtful—this was a Kyriakis tradition he intended to break with.

'At another time I'd love to hear your views on modern parenting, but...'

Beth compressed her lips and thought *sarcastic rat*. 'I suppose *you'd* say it made you the man you are.'

A man perfectly suited to the brutal cut-throat world he operated in—great at work, hopeless in relationships. She knew the kind; well, not personally, obviously, but you only had to look at him to know he was not a giver, though very possibly good in bed?

The uncensored maverick addition made her eyes widen in alarm.

'No, actually, I agree with you.'

'What about?' Calm down—there is no way he can know you were wondering what he was like in bed.

'It is a totally barbaric practice; I would never do that to my son.' And you told her this why, exactly?

'Your son?' Beth echoed in surprise, even as she instantly envisaged a baby with golden skin and dark hair lying in her arms, looking up at her with Theo's eyes.

She blinked hard to banish the image. Of course he was going to have children; why was the idea so startling? And why had she seen herself holding his baby?

'Kyriakis tradition does not consider it so important for daughters to develop toughness and independence while still in the womb.'

'So their role is to have babies.'

'And look decorative,' Theo added, deadpan. 'But there were just the three of us, no girls.'

'Three?' she exclaimed, momentarily sidetracked. It was the first she had heard of another brother.

She saw something flicker at the back of his eyes but there was no trace of emotion in Theo's voice as he said, 'Niki was the eldest; he died the year I was sent to prep school.' Where his guilt had remained unexpressed and his silent grief for the big brother he had worshipped had been interpreted as truculence.

'Andreas never mentioned him.' This surprised her as he spoke about Theo all the time.

In fact the number of times he came into the conversation—*Theo this, Theo that*—had been irritating the hell out of Beth for years; it made her angry to know that Andreas had spent his life living in his big brother's shadow.

'Is there any reason he should have?' When they had been growing up, if anyone mentioned their brother's name their father would retreat to his study for days at a time. In later years, it had become an unspoken rule within the family that his name was not mentioned; this had not changed, even after their father's death.

'Because I'm just the PA?'

He viewed her with narrow-eyed irritation. 'Do you have to be so defensive? That chip on your shoulder is not attractive.'

Beth ignored the chip jibe, levelled a sweet smile at his face and said, 'When the alternative is agreeing with everything you say—yes.'

'My brother did not mention an event that happened when he was little more than a baby; I would not read too much into it. A man does not feel the need to reveal every microscopic detail about himself, though when you are together I'm sure he will bare his soul to you,' he said sardonically, wondering if the female existed who did not feel the need to delve into every corner of a man's life from his politics to childhood traumas.

'You did.'

'I—' Theo stopped, an arrested expression spreading across his dark features as he realised she was right.

A flicker of wariness appeared in his eyes as he met Beth Farley's challenging gaze. After a six month mutually pleasing arrangement, the last woman he had slept with, the divine and work-orientated Camilla, had known little about his personal likes and dislikes outside the bedroom and he had felt no impulse whatever to reveal them.

Not that it was a totally equal comparison. Elizabeth Farley was *not* the woman in his life, though, possibly, considering his growing fascination with her sulky sexy mouth, he should find a replacement for Camilla.

His brother's assistant was just a good listener, which was why he chose women who were interested in very little other than themselves—you knew exactly where you were with egocentric, beautiful women. It was the warm, fluffy ones oozing empathy you had to view with suspicion—they were the ones who morphed into bunny-boilers when you rejected their devotion.

They did not understand the meaning or the advantages of keeping things light.

Theo drew their conversation to a close by withdrawing a phone from his pocket and selecting a number. While he was waiting for someone to pick up, he consulted his watch. 'It's eleven now; that gives us eight hours.'

'Eight hours to what?'

'To make you the woman of my brother's dreams.'

Beth, who had thought she might buy a new dress on the way home, stared. 'What are you talking about?'

He waved her silent and spoke into the receiver. 'Nicola… no, leave that today. I have a job for you.' He glanced towards Beth and added, 'It won't be easy, but I think you're up to it.'

Beth watched, her blood quietly simmering, while he got to his feet, walked across to the other side of the room and began to pace up and down as he spoke, issuing a number of terse instructions, reminding her as he did so of some lithe, sleek jungle predator. He was a total pain but, aesthetically speaking, there was no denying he was also pretty riveting to watch.

Theo returned a moment later. 'Right, that's organised.'

'What's organised?' Beth's enthusiasm for the project was cooling in direct proportion to his zeal. You'll never know if you don't try, reminded the voice in her head.

'An appointment at the spa for a bit of pampering.' He left the details to Nicola, who, he was sure, knew all there was to know about female grooming. 'Hair, make-up, a suitable outfit.'

As she listened, Beth's wariness grew. It was one thing to fantasise about blowing Andreas away with her stunning beauty but this wasn't fantasy, it was real, and she could see several flaws in his plan.

He walked purposefully towards the door, clearly expecting her to follow. When she made no attempt to move, he turned, his broad brow pleated in a frown. 'Is there a problem?'

Other than you being the rudest, most manipulative man on the planet? 'I have a stack of work to do. I can't walk out in the middle of the morning.'

'Your dedication does you credit but, as the person paying your salary, I give you permission to leave early. In fact, I insist upon it.'

The smooth rejoinder made Beth frown darkly. 'Until I leave, Andreas pays my salary,' she said, not budging. 'And, anyway, how long can it take to get ready?' Usually, she allowed herself ten minutes.

'I pay Andreas's salary,' he said, walking across to her desk and, with an end-of-the-story gesture, he depressed the switch on her laptop. 'And if you do what I say, you won't need to leave.'

Beth's angry eyes flew to his. 'This is not going to work and we both know it.'

'Do you want to spend the rest of your life wondering what if?' he goaded softly. 'Or are you the sort of girl who finds her own white charger and goes to rescue her prince?'

Beth shook her head. 'You are one manipulative...' She bit her tongue and eyed him with narrow-eyed dislike. 'If I wasn't a nice girl...'

He laughed down into her angry, flushed face. '*Nice* has a limited appeal for men, Elizabeth.'

'Not all men are as disgusting as you.'

'I think you will find they actually are, Elizabeth. Now, let's leave *nice*. I think it is your other...*qualities* that need some work.'

Beth planted her hands on her hips and, tapping a foot on the wooden floor, stuck out her chin. 'Don't start minding my feelings now; if you're trying to say I'm not sexy, go ahead,' she invited. 'It's not exactly news to me.'

There was a gleam in his eyes that Beth found most disturbing as his glance slid down the length of her body before returning to her face.

'Now that,' he approved, 'is a good look for you. Just carry on thinking what you are now and we're halfway there.'

'I'm thinking you are a hateful creep!'

The mocking glint in his dark eyes deepened. 'Why, Elizabeth, you're fighting it but I think you're starting to like me.'

'Sure, you're my hero.'

CHAPTER FIVE

BETH, her attention on the tall svelte blonde who Theo had introduced simply as Nicola, didn't register the long low limo until the gleaming monster had pulled up literally beside her.

The uniformed driver got out and opened the door for her.

Was she meant to get in? Beth paused uncertainly and glanced towards Theo—no help there; his attention was on his companion.

They certainly made a striking couple.

It occurred to Beth that Theo's plan might have stood a better chance of working if he had chosen a woman like Nicola to seduce Andreas... Actually, now that she thought about it, why not choose Nicola?

From what she'd seen so far, it didn't seem likely that any request he made would receive a negative response—the woman acted as if she'd do anything for her boss.

Maybe he was more than a boss?

The possibility—no, cancel that, *probability*—introduced a cynical twist to Beth's reflective smile. Not that it was anything to do with her if they were sleeping together, though it did strike her as rather unprofessional.

One advantage of looking the way she did was that no one had ever accused her of sleeping her way to the top, not that she was at the top or even halfway there. Actually, she wasn't sure how far up the ladder she wanted to go.

She had more fallen into her career than planned it. Sometimes she asked herself what she was doing with her life, then she got her pay cheque and thought that so long as she could pay the bills it didn't really matter.

Smiling at the driver, Beth slid inside. 'Crikey!' She saw the driver grin at her involuntary exclamation and wiped the expression of wide-eyed wonder from her face. 'Very nice,' she added in a bored drawl, trying, and she suspected failing, to give the impression that she was accustomed to this sort of opulence.

If she didn't want to come over as terminally gauche Beth realised she really would have to watch the wide-eyed wonder stuff.

When, a moment later, willowy Nicola in her figure-enhancing black jacket, miniskirt and thigh-high boots joined her, Theo had vanished. As the car drew away from the kerb, Beth was unable to keep a lid on her misgivings.

'I'm not sure this is a good idea.' Not a good idea? It was total and absolute insanity. She wondered what would happen if she demanded they stop the car, but something stopped her from finding out.

The thought that Theo might be right and Andreas might notice her.

'Relax,' her companion advised. 'Enjoy.' She tilted her head to study Beth's face and observed with a note of surprise, 'Theo's right—your face does have potential.' She drew out the word thoughtfully and reached out a hand to brush the hair back from Beth's brow.

Beth jerked away from the clinical contact. 'Would you like me to show you my teeth too?' she asked, baring them in a white gritted smile, the thought of two people who could stop conversation simply by walking into a room discussing her looks or, rather, lack thereof was utterly mortifying.

The other woman looked startled and then laughed.

'You were talking about me?' Beth began angrily, then stopped, realising the stupidity of the question. Considering the context of the situation, it was obvious they'd been discussing her.

'It's a pity you're not taller but...' Without finishing the observation, Nicola settled back in her seat and, producing a compact from her bag, began to reapply the scarlet outline of her lips.

Beth watched her, realising that, despite her initial impression, the other woman was not beautiful but she was striking.

Striking, poised, polished and confident.

What was her relationship with her employer? Just how close were they?

An image flashed, unbidden, into Beth's head. She blinked to banish the shocking impression of long limbs entwined and glistening skin and shook her head to drive away the soft moans and fragmented gasps whispering in her ears.

Lifting a hand to her burning cheeks, Beth experienced a twinge of envy, not, *obviously*, because the older woman might be sleeping with her boss—for that, in her opinion, the other woman would deserve her deepest sympathy—it was the other woman's poise and confidence she envied.

The statuesque blonde smiled complacently at her reflection and clicked her compact closed, finally satisfied with the reapplication of colour. She lifted a hand to the razor-cropped bleached hair and turned her attention back to Beth.

'Relax—this is going to be fun.'

Easy for you to say, Beth thought, directing a cranky look at her travelling companion, though she knew her annoyance was directed at the wrong person.

'Not my idea of fun.'

The other woman shrugged and, miming a *sorry*, took the ringing phone from her jacket. She listened for a moment and then said, 'No, that won't do at all.' She closed her eyes and, for the space of several minutes, listened in silence before issuing a hissing sound of annoyance from between her clenched white teeth and saying sarcastically, 'Would you like to tell him that? No, I thought not.' She spent the next few minutes with the phone welded to her ear, speaking intermittently before finally closing it and sliding it back into her pocket. 'Sorry about that.'

'Was that...him?'

'Theo?'

Beth took the amused laughter as a *no* and asked, 'Have you worked for...him long?'

'Theo, you mean?'

Beth nodded and wondered why she was so reluctant to say the man's name.

'Three years.'

'I've been working for Andreas for three years too, but of course I'm just a secretary.'

'There is no such thing as *just* a secretary.'

Beth rolled her eyes and said, 'Let me guess—a Theo quote?' If he lost his billions he could always take up motivational speaking, she thought sourly.

The other woman grinned and shrugged. 'Actually, I was a secretary too.'

Beth's eyes widened. 'I assumed that you were some sort of fast track graduate.' The Kyriakis organisation had the pick of the crop of new talent emerging from all the top universities and the competition for graduate places in every department, from legal to finance, was intense.

'No, I was never what you'd call academic, and now…' she mused, casting a knowing look at Beth's face. 'You're thinking I slept my way to the top, or at least halfway up?' she speculated, looking more amused than annoyed.

'No, really, I…' Beth lied guiltily.

'My previous boss used to pat me on the head and then take the credit for my ideas.'

Beth, who caught herself nodding sympathetically in response to this change of subject, stopped and said defensively, 'Andreas isn't like that.'

'Glad to hear it, but I wasn't so lucky and when I got sent to cover for Theo's PA when she was out sick I expected more of the same from him.'

'But you didn't get it?' Beth asked, curious in spite of herself. In-house gossip on Theo was confusing; people said he was impossibly demanding, but Beth had noticed that these people were not the ones who worked directly with him. Those people tended to be incredibly loyal…or maybe they were too scared to complain?

She had always assumed the latter but she had to admit that Nicola did not act like someone who was downtrodden and intimidated.

'No.'

'But I thought—' Beth's glance fell from the other woman's bright blue gaze and she shook her head and mumbled, 'Forget it.'

'That he is impossibly demanding and difficult?' The tall blonde gave a husky chuckle. 'He is both,' she admitted cheerfully. 'He pushes himself hard and he expects the same level of commitment from others, but he's generous and a great teacher.' She gave a sly grin and added innocently, 'But maybe you know that already?'

Beth looked at her blankly. 'I don't understand...' the penny dropped and she stopped dead, the colour flying to her cheeks. 'No, I don't.'

Close or not, it would seem that Theo had only told this woman the details he considered she needed to know. It came as no surprise to learn that he was not big on explaining himself.

'Calm down!' Nicola soothed. 'I was just asking.' Her glance skimmed over Beth and she added, 'Though you're not really his type.'

'You mean I'm not eye candy.'

Just because this woman painted Theo as some progressive saintlike boss, it didn't mean he was. If she was sleeping with her boss, she was not going to tell people he was hell to work for.

'You *really* like him?'

Beth's incredulity appeared to amuse the other woman. 'Theo Kyriakis is one of the few men I know who isn't threatened by intelligent women. If you get the chance to work for him,' she continued seriously, 'go for it. He is seriously a great teacher.'

The idea of being taught anything by Theo Kyriakis made a shudder of distaste trace a shaky path down her spine. 'I really don't think that's going to happen.'

The other woman shrugged. 'No, you're probably right; he doesn't mix business and pleasure.'

The mortified colour flew to Beth's cheeks. 'God, no, it's not like that.'

'Not my business,' said the blonde cheerfully. 'But, if you are looking for a job, I'm ready to fly the coop. He's offered me the New York office, but I'm not so sure,' she revealed with surprising candour.

'I thought you were his assistant.'

'I am—or I was; Theo likes to work with people he thinks have potential.'

Beth, who had heard enough about perfect boss Theo, released a slow, cleansing breath and changed the subject—anything but Theo Kyriakis was fine by her. 'Where are we going?'

'The spa is our first stop... You're booked in for the usual suspects.'

Beth, who hadn't a clue what the *usual suspects* entailed, nodded.

'I could do with a massage myself,' Nicola mused, rotating her shoulders. 'But no time,' she added regretfully.

'You probably think this is odd?'

The blonde's pencilled brows rose. 'Theo always has a reason and if he wants me to know he tells me; if not...' She looked at Beth and shrugged.

The spa turned out to be every bit as luxurious as Beth had anticipated, but the afternoon of pampering and relaxation she had expected never really happened.

From the moment she arrived she was organised with military precision, attacked from all sides by a stream of professionals who all had a *no pain, no gain* mentality.

When Nicola returned two hours later she been buffed, polished and clipped within an inch of her life.

'So how was that?' Nicola asked.

'I had no idea that grooming could be so painful. If anyone comes within fifty yards of me with wax again I will prosecute. It is assault,' Beth told her bitterly.

Nicola looked sympathetic. 'Don't worry, you've only got hair and nails left—that's relatively painless.'

'This is a salon?' Beth said, shading her eyes as she stared up at the impressive façade of the Georgian terrace they had just stopped in front of.

'It's not a salon; it's Theo's London place. Have you never been here?'

Beth shook her head and thought *I don't want to be here now.*

'The stylists are here.'

'I was expecting…' She stopped, shook her head and heaved a sigh—why waste her breath?

It was fast becoming obvious that her expectations were not of any real importance—what Theo wanted, Theo got.

'I don't suppose I have any say in the matter.' Beth caught the other woman looking at her oddly and forced a smile. 'Come on then, let's get it over with,' she said gloomily as she approached the building with the enthusiasm of a condemned woman.

CHAPTER SIX

THEO, who had been drumming his fingers on the desk, stopped as the door opened. He saw Nicola standing there and frowned.

'I said have her ready for seven.'

Nicola glanced at her watch. 'It's only a quarter after.'

'The clock is still ticking. How long does it take to cut a woman's hair and put her in some clothes? I would have thought...' He broke off and frowned as the intrusive sound of the army of stylists exiting noisily in the hallway drowned him out.

'She's still upstairs.'

Theo hid his frustration behind a stony expression. 'Why?'

Nicola held up her hands. 'Look, don't blame the messenger. I tried, I really did, but your Beth is not what you'd call a big entrance girl.'

'What are you talking about?'

'Your date won't come out—a first for you...?' she observed, trying to disguise her amusement.

A sound of irritation emerged from between Theo's clenched teeth. 'So she's hiding in the bedroom. Presumably the makeover was not a success.'

'The makeover was...'

'What colour did they put her in?'

'Black.'

Theo clicked his tongue with exasperation. 'I *expressly* said she needed some colour.'

'You did,' Nicola agreed calmly.

'The woman spends her life in dull colours.' Black would drain her already pale skin and make her look more colourless than ever. Even he knew that and no one was paying him to know about fashion.

Nicola stopped as Theo held up his hand.

'All right, I get the picture, but she can't look *that* bad.' If the girl had unrealistic expectations it was not his fault. *You raised her expectations* said the voice in his head.

'Well, actually she—' Nicola found herself talking to thin air. She reached the hallway in time to see her boss gain the top of the curving flight of stairs.

Theo made a quick detour into his own dressing room, grabbed a fresh shirt and tie from the nest rack of similar items and, shrugging himself out of the one he'd been wearing all day, left the room.

He banged on the door before barging in, stopping dead when he found the room empty.

'Go away!'

The small voice came from the adjoining bathroom.

'Come out, Beth.' He struggled to inject a coaxing note into his voice. Female dramatics did not amuse him. Less still did the feeling of guilt he could not shake.

Inside the bathroom, Beth shook her head, then stopped as her new hairstyle bounced before settling back into place.

She had been unable to contain her disquiet as the drifts of shorn hair on the floor became a deep soft pile.

'I don't really think short hair suits me.'

We have kept most of the length, the man who called himself simply Anton had explained, conveying the strong impression as he did so that he was not accustomed to defending his artistic efforts.

When he had finished, the loose curls down her back did still reach her shoulder blades but it didn't stop Beth feeling naked and exposed—though not, obviously, as exposed as this dress made her feel—with the heavy, long hair around her face reduced to feathery tendrils.

Both he and the make-up artist had raved about her cheekbones and said it was criminal that she had been hiding them.

Theo leaned his shoulders on the wall and consulted his watch. 'What do you intend to do? Stay in there for ever?'

Beth turned on the tap to drown out his voice. She could think of worse ideas at that moment than never leaving the bathroom, and a person could actually live for a long time on water and she had plenty of that. She dabbed a wet tissue to her lips and scrubbed hard. The colour stubbornly stayed put; it didn't even smudge.

Beth leaned on the wall and, close to panic, shut her eyes. She took a deep breath—this was ludicrous, but not life-threatening.

She walked over to the mirror and stared at her reflection. *No, it's not ludicrous, but I am, for getting sucked into this entire Cinderella scenario.*

Theo had dangled a carrot and she had fallen for the bait.

The hair, the make-up, even the clothes, she thought, glancing down at the close-fitting black sheath that clung to her waist and hips like a second skin before flaring out from the knee—they had all been part of the bait.

'Well…?'

Ignoring the impatient voice on the other side of the door, Beth turned her back on the person staring back at her from the mirror; it was bizarre to see a stranger looking back at her. What she needed was an industrial cleaner to get this stuff off her face and her own clothes.

Her clothes were in the other room. 'I'm not coming out while you're there.'

She heard him snap out an expletive before he finally said, 'Fine. I have to go to meet them now; stay there if you want to.'

And, after a few moments, she heard the door open and then close. Beth listened, unable to believe it had been that easy...before she cautiously opened the bathroom door.

Other than the racks of designer garments and rows of shoes that the hit team from the exclusive department store had left behind, the room was empty. With a sigh of relief, she ran over to the bed to retrieve her own clothes.

Only they were not where she had left them. Instead, there was a crumpled shirt and tie that she would have sworn had not been there before.

'Where on earth?' she mumbled, pulling aside the quilt to look beneath it.

'Looking for these?'

With a startled gasp, Beth swung around, straightening up just as a tall figure re-entered the room. He was holding the neat stack of her clothes, which he dropped on the floor before beginning to casually button the shirt that hung open to his waist, revealing the ridged muscles of his flat belly and a teasing glimpse of the light dusting of body hair on his golden chest.

Beth's eyes made an unscheduled journey from his face to his waist as a silent shiver that began low in her pelvis rippled outwards until her entire body was involved.

She took a deep breath and dragged her eyes upwards. So Theo Kyriakis was in pretty good shape—this was not exactly news.

Actually, *pretty good* might, she conceded, be the under-statement of the century. He had the sort of body fantasies were made of, though not, obviously, her own.

Theo had been annoyed his plan had gone pear-shaped but prepared to cut her some slack. It wasn't her fault that things hadn't worked and he was actually reasonably philo-sophical about the failure.

But he had been surprised. Theo considered himself a pretty good judge of such things and he had been sure that Elizabeth Farley would scrub up pretty well; of course he hadn't been expecting miracles or a wow, stop-in-your-tracks moment.

His expectations had been much more realistic, but he had genuinely thought that getting her out of those drab clothes would be a vast improvement and a bit of gloss to draw attention to those lush, seductive lips would make any man forget her less than classical features.

An image of that mouth was drifting through his mind as she whipped around to face him, her newly styled hair fanning out like a silky cloud around her face before settling in silky waves down her back.

Theo got the wow moment he had not been anticipating—it hit him like a fist connecting with his solar plexus.

A husky expletive slipped unnoticed from his lips as he drew a deep breath; he had no more control over his body than an adolescent in the first grip of lust as he stood there, nailed to the spot, and stared.

He had, admittedly, thought she had potential but not this! Who knew that under the frumpy suits and high-but-toned collars was a body that any woman would trade her entire collection of designer handbags for, and any man… he shook his head slightly and exhaled the air that had been trapped in his lungs in one long sigh and thought…any man, including his brother, would want to possess.

The mystery was why any woman would hide a body like that.

And, despite his misgivings, the black had not turned out to be a mistake, he conceded, sending up a silent apology to the stylists who, it turned out, did know their job. The stark column of black brought out the opalescent sheen of her pale creamy skin and the loose, low cowl neckline of the dress revealed the beauty of her lovely neck and shoulders while offering tantalising little glimpses of her small high breasts when she moved.

'You said you'd go,' Beth accused, directing a bitter look at his face.

Theo didn't respond. He just carried on staring at her with a fixed intensity that she found unnerving; if she had felt self-conscious and awkward previously in the unaccustomed finery, now his reaction made her feel a million times worse.

It wasn't until she heard his startled exclamation of dismay—that Beth realised that she had still, in one stubbornly optimistic corner of her brain, nurtured a faint hope that she was overreacting. A man with an ounce of sensitivity would have hidden his disappointment, she reflected bitterly.

'Well, now you know,' she said, lifting her arms wide and performing a shaky twirl, the accompanying laugh emerging as a rusty croak. 'Sorry.'

'Sorry?'

There was an oddly blank look in his eyes as they connected with her own; they were so dark that it was impossible to tell where the pupil ended. The effect was strangely hypnotic.

The nerve-shredding awkward silence stretched.

What else was she meant to say? she wondered as she finally wrenched her eyes from his; she only made it as far as his sternly sensual mouth and the muscle that was clenching beside it.

He was clearly really aggravated that his plan had fallen apart at the first hurdle. It had not even occurred to him to consider how she might be feeling… No, of course it hadn't. My God, he had to be the most egocentric and selfish man on the planet!

The resentment inside her suddenly exploded. 'Don't look at me like that—it's not my fault!' she yclled.

'There is no need to raise your voice.' His eyes slid to her heaving breasts. Andreas's eyes were going to pop out of his head when he saw her.

This transformation worked on many levels. His brother was going to be kicking himself that this woman had been sitting a few feet away from him for years and he was going to be consumed with jealousy because she was with Theo.

'Actually, there is a need. *I* told you it was a ridiculous idea, but you would have it your way, as usual…' Breathing hard through flared nostrils, she planted her hands on her hips, unwittingly causing the fabric of her dress to pull tight across her breasts, and fixed him with a resentful glare. 'Do you ever listen to anyone else? Silly question; of course you don't. Well, for the record, I know I look ridiculous so I don't need you to tell me.' Or look at me as if I've grown a second head.

She wrapped her arms across her chest in a protective gesture and wished he'd stop staring. 'And don't you dare tell me to put a positive slant on it,' she warned him darkly.

'All right, I won't,' Theo agreed, adjusting the knot of his tie.

'Because I'm up to here,' she informed him, raising her hand a foot above her head, 'with being positive and putting a brave face on it when life actually sucks.' She paused to catch her breath and thought this was definitely one of those life-sucking moments. 'A slutty dress,' she observed bitterly, 'is not going to change the fact I'm just not eye candy material.'

Hearing the self-pitying quiver in her voice, she lifted her chin and thought, live with it, Beth, you weren't some sexy siren when you got out of bed this morning so, actually, nothing has changed.

'The dress is not slutty.'

'You mean I am?' she queried sharply.

A shadow of impatience moved across Theo's face. 'Don't be ridiculous.'

'I'm simply not sexy,' she added, unable to shake free of the self-pitying mode.

Any sexier and she would need to carry a government health warning. 'The dress,' he said, struggling for patience, 'is not *slutty*; it is classy and sexy.' And she was clearly certifiable if she truly had no inkling of how she looked.

'Oh, I'm sure it cost a lot of money,' she admitted, stretching out a leg to examine the effect as the folds of fabric pulled tight against her thigh. She pointed her toe and, thinking of the hand-sewn label she had spotted, admitted, 'I'm sure it would look tremendous on someone who could carry it off.' And someone with less in the breasts department; the lift effect of the boned bodice and loose cowl neckline was alarming, she decided, squinting down at of the amount of cleavage on display.

'Why can you not carry it off?' Theo asked.

Assuming he was joking, she gave a snort of laughter.

'If you're worried about the money...' Beth grimaced. She wouldn't blame him if he was; there hadn't been a single price tag on any of the outfits hanging on the rail they'd wheeled in but she was pretty sure any one would have cost more than her yearly clothing budget '…I'm sure they'll take the dress and the other things back.'

Which would leave her wearing very little. Without warning, a picture formed in his head to illustrate the point; he saw her standing there minus the slinky dress, and in his expert opinion, she was not wearing a bra.

It took him the space of several heartbeats before he could banish the steamy, distracting image.

'Just what is your problem?'

Honesty prevented Beth from yelling *I'm looking at it*, because he hadn't made her spend the day being pampered and primped. But it was tempting, really tempting.

What he had done was what he did best—he had exploited her weakness, *made* her do this.

Why would any woman hide a body like that? he wondered as his gaze moved over the slender female curves. Her breasts were surprisingly full, her hips narrow by contrast and her waist incredibly narrow; her slim hips had a deliciously feminine flare.

'Or maybe you could get someone my size to take my place—' Beth suggested hopefully.

'Enough!'

The sharp command cut her off. Beth opened her mouth to protest, then, as her eyes moved from his sensually moulded mouth to his eyes, she stopped abruptly. Something kicked low in her belly, her eyes connected with his hooded stare and a little shiver trickled down her spine.

'Thank you,' he murmured ironically.

The silence between them ticked on for another few uncomfortable moments before he dragged a hand back and forth across his dark hair, rumpling it and making it stand up spikily at the front.

'You should consider professional help with your body issues, but I am not a therapist.'

'No, you're the big boss.'

'You don't seem impressed?'

'Of course I'm impressed. You sit at a big desk that is never untidy because you don't do any work—you just make decisions. Which I am sure is very difficult,' she jeered.

The breath whistled through his clenched teeth. 'I have had a very trying day and my patience is limited. It might not be a good idea to wind me up, Elizabeth.'

Beth flung up her hands in an attitude of utter frustration. '*You've* had a trying day?' My God, she had not credited him with a sympathetic nature but, even by his egocentric standards, this statement struck her as incredibly selfish. 'Have you been sitting there all afternoon while people poke, prod, peel and act like you're some sort of freak of nature? My skin is wrong, my hair is wrong, my...'

Without any warning, he took her chin between his thumb and forefinger and tilted her face up to him. Beth froze, her mouth half open, her pupils dilating as she lifted her eyes to meet his.

A slow insolent smile tugged at the corners of his sensual mouth but his dark eyes stayed sombre as he ran a finger slowly down the curve of her cheek.

Beth had no control over the shiver that ran through her body in response to the light touch. Mouth dry, she swallowed. Her heart was thudding, the charge in the air made it hard for her to catch her breath.

'If they criticised your skin, they are fools,' he pronounced, rubbing the pad of his thumb along her jaw. 'It is perfect and flawless like silk.' His lifted his hand and pushed his long fingers in her hair, an expression that had all the hallmarks of compulsion sliding into his eyes as his fingertips grazed her scalp.

Beth flinched and pulled back, shocked clear of the creeping paralysis that had nailed her to the spot by the shock of the electric surge that tingled along her nerve endings.

'Nothing I say will convince you that you look fantastic, will it?' His questioning gaze swept across her flushed upturned features.

She shook her head and watched the annoyance and frustration flash in his eyes. Breathing fast and uncomfortably conscious of the heat low in her belly, Beth ran her tongue across her lips, unwittingly drawing his attention to the soft curve.

Unable to explain the physical effect he had on her, she lifted her chin and took a casual step backwards.

Foiling her attempt to regain some personal space, he shadowed her action and then took another step, standing way too close. She couldn't think; she couldn't breathe.

'I thought not.' His thumb skimmed lightly over the curve of her cheek before he slid his fingers down the pale column of her neck; he could feel the vibration of the pulse at the base of her throat through his fingertips.

His touch was light. There was nothing stopping her just stepping away, but she didn't; the powerful aura of raw sexuality he radiated froze her to the spot. She had never been physically aware of a man the way she was of Theo.

The seething intensity in his stare made her shiver. His dark sensual gaze sealed to her face, he curved a hand across her behind and pulled her into his body. Beth lifted her hands to push him away but somehow they stayed where they were against his chest. Palms flat, she spread her fingers, conscious as she did so of the hard solidity of his chest, the heat of his skin and the vibration of his strong beating heart.

Her own heart was acting like a captured bird throwing itself against her ribcage.

The corners of his sensual mouth tugged upwards in a

smile that spelt danger as Theo reached his other hand to cup the back of her head.

She swallowed past the emotional thickness aching in her throat and opened her mouth a split second before Theo covered it with his own.

Shock held her immobile.

Eyes wide, she stood there while his lips settled against her own, then, as his tongue slid between her parted lips, her eyes drifted shut. Without knowing how it happened, she was kissing him back, her arms curved around his neck as her feet left the floor. Above the roaring in her ears she heard a soft fractured moan but did not associate it with herself.

When he released her Beth took a staggering step backwards, batting away the steadying hand he extended as she wiped a hand across her trembling mouth. The seductive mixture of passion and dazed shock in her glazed eyes made Theo want to kiss her again.

'Was that actually necessary?' she asked, even as she asked herself how she had come to be kissing him back. He wasn't Andreas; she didn't even like him.

'I think so,' he responded calmly. 'Do you believe me now that you look incredible?'

She blinked. 'You kissed me to—' It was an explanation, but not one that explained the raw driving need she had glimpsed in his face.

'I kissed you because you weren't listening.' It did not seem necessary to add that he had wanted to kiss her, that the idea of doing so had been growing all day until it had become a constant distraction.

It had been a two birds with one stone situation—satisfy his curiosity and remove the distraction.

In theory, at least.

'The only thing you proved is that you know how to kiss, though, frankly, given your press, I was expecting better.'

There was a short startled silence before he burst out laughing. 'Andreas will spontaneously combust when he sees you in that dress.'

She stared at him, her frown morphing into a wary smile. 'Seriously?'

'Seriously,' he agreed drily.

Beth gazed at him in amazement and said cautiously. 'You really *like* the way I look?'.

He dragged a brown hand over his dark hair and looked exasperated. 'I thought I had already demonstrated that. Perhaps I am losing my knack.'

'Oh, no, you're not.' Blushing fierily the moment the uncensored and heartfelt words left her lips, Beth willed the floor at her feet to open up.

'It is not me you need to drive wild with lust.' *Wild* was a slight overstatement, he told himself, because he was still in control.

Control was not a problem for him.

The derision in his tone brought a mortified flush to her cheeks. 'That would be a nightmare.' Not to mention about as probable as her being offered the lead in a West End musical—she was tone deaf.

As her antagonistic gaze slid to his mouth, Beth was conscious of a tight fist of heat low in her stomach as her eyes traced the sensual curve. She lowered her glance quickly, catching her full lip between her teeth—she refused to think *wild* and *lust* in the same sentence as Theo Kyriakis!

It was just too uncomfortable.

The woman who did drive this man *wild with lust* had her total sympathy because the impeccable tailoring and cultured aloof manner was only a thin veneer; peel it away and Beth was pretty sure that on a sexual level he was not the sort of man who held back and being on the receiving end of all that raw sexuality…?

Beth gave a little shudder. Some women might find the dark, brooding stuff exciting but she was definitely not one of them; she'd prefer to plug herself into a million volts of neat electricity and half suspected the effect would be much the same.

'I was simply asking for the male viewpoint; you are a man.' She blinked as her eyes connected with his and thought, actually, he was probably more masculine than any other man on the planet! 'I've no desire to send anyone wild with lust,' she promised him truthfully.

All the same, it was hard not to wonder what Theo would look like in the grip of uncontrollable lust. The kiss had been controlled, devastating but basically a means of proving a point.

It had proved he was a very good kisser but with that mouth it had always been sort of a given.

Without warning, Theo leaned towards her and Beth pushed the maverick thought away as she took a step backwards and collided with a chair; it fell over with a clatter and she would have overbalanced if he hadn't shot out a hand to steady her.

'You can't pull away when I touch you,' he warned irritably.

'Why would you touch me?' And would touching include more kissing? Her sensitive stomach muscles flipped at the prospect.

'Because the more I touch you, the more *I* find you fascinating and the more Andreas will want to touch you too and the more Ariana will want to scratch your eyes out.'

The groove above his aquiline nose deepened as he studied the smooth skin of her face. He had not anticipated this degree of success, or the very real probability that Ariana's anger might be aimed at her made-over rival. Theo was becoming uneasily aware that Elizabeth Farley was not equipped to deal with the likes of Ariana.

He pushed away the unease and reminded himself that he would be there to act as a buffer and keep Ariana in line.

'I'm glad you think it's funny.' Even as she spoke, she realised he had stopped smiling and was looking pretty grim.

'Don't worry. I will protect you.'

Her gaze drifted to his mouth and Beth experienced a scary little rush of excitement. 'And who is going to protect me from you?'

He gave a sardonic smile. 'Andreas—isn't that the whole point of this?'

She moved and caught sight of her reflection in the full-length mirror. Panic shot through her and she suddenly felt as if there was a heavy weight pressing down on her chest and she couldn't breathe.

She covered her face with her hands. 'I'm beginning to wonder if there ever was a point to any of this.'

'Don't bail out on me now, Elizabeth.' He could literally see the throb of her heartbeat beneath the black silk. 'What's the worst that can happen?' he asked, pitching his voice low as if he were soothing a nervous horse.

Some of the calm in his voice seeped into Beth. She dropped her hands, exhaled and lifted her chin. Her gran had never had much sympathy for any kind of cowardice.

Though Beth doubted Gran had had this situation in mind when she had advised facing your fears.

She gave him a direct look. 'The worst already has happened.'

He arched a dark questioning brow.

A distracted expression fogged Beth's angry gaze as the memories intruded; for one brief moment inside her head she could taste him, feel him, smell… She drew a shaky inhalation, wiped a hand across her lips and pushed away the images.

His grin flashed, though it did not reach his eyes as he recalled the soft lost cry she had moaned into his mouth. 'There you go—it's all up from here on in.'

'I wish I could share your optimism,' she said, thinking that life had been far simpler when she had been unable to recognise the charm in Theo Kyriakis's smile.

CHAPTER SEVEN

BETH was silent on the journey to the restaurant but it was clear to Theo that she was bursting to say something.

He unbuckled his seat belt and turned to her; the woman was hard work. 'All right; spit it out.'

'There's one thing you haven't considered,' she said, looking worried.

'I doubt that.'

His confidence irritated her. 'Why—because you always think of everything?' His conceit really was incredible.

'Not on this occasion, it would seem,' he said, looking at her soft pink mouth and feeling a strong urge to kiss her again; this fixation was a possibility he had not considered.

'While you're pretending to...to...' He arched a questioning brow and she glared at him and said angrily, 'Fancy me.'

Her gruff embarrassment drew a laugh from Theo and the need to kiss her intensified.

She slung him a look of angry reproach. 'What about your girlfriend—how is she going to feel? I know it's acting, but will she?'

'I do not encourage jealousy in my girlfriends.'

Beth rolled her eyes. No, she thought, he encouraged long

legs and cut glass profiles. Maybe it was a genetic thing, she mused gloomily. Andreas went for much the same.

Though their tastes did differ in one significant area. Theo Kyriakis, if his brother and the things she'd read were accurate, appeared to date almost exclusively high achievers, successful in their own field, women in high profile jobs who were sophisticated and stylish—none of them looked the needy type.

Andreas, on the other hand, didn't seem to mind needy so long as the needy female in question greeted every comment he made with breathless wonder and told him he was marvellous.

Shocked by the disloyal direction of her thoughts, Beth scowled.

'Whether you encourage it or not, there is no way your girlfriend is going to be happy if she finds out you've been… flirting with me.'

'If it makes you any happier, there is no girlfriend at present.' And there hadn't been for three months, which might account for the difficulty he was having keeping his mind off the idea of kissing her again.

Her eyes flew wide. *'Seriously?'* She shook her head, her brows twitching into a straight line. 'Why?' His expression made her realise that she was trespassing in areas that were none of her business, though, in justification, he did not feel similarly inhibited when it came to delving into her personal affairs—such as they were.

'Sorry, it's none of my business, it just seemed a bit—'

He regarded her with a satirical glint in his dark eyes and prompted, 'A bit…?'

'Well, if you must know—odd.'

'Why would it be *odd* that I have no woman in my—'

As he was speaking, a distracting image drifted through

her head and, without thinking, Beth voiced the basic content, 'Bed.'

His brows lifted towards his dark hairline. 'Life.'

Beth flushed at the dry rebuttal and bit her lip.

There was a speculative gleam in his eyes as he watched her, running his hand back and forth across his short hair. 'You appear a little fixated on my sex life, Elizabeth.'

An accusation that was hard for her to deny—though she fully intended to—maybe this sort of thing happened to any female who lingered too long this close to that aura of raw sex he projected, even when his hair was sticking up spikily.

Beth experienced a sudden strong urge to smooth down those dark strands. Instead, she picked up a glossy magazine from a holder and began to flick through it.

'We are not talking platonic relationships or a meeting of minds.' The graphic images of his naked body were a product of a sick mind—*hers*! 'And don't call me *Elizabeth*,' she added, a hint of desperation creeping into her voice.

'It suits you,' he pronounced, studying her face as she caught her lower lip between her teeth. Her wide eyes were wary; the flush of colour along her cheekbones emphasised the delicate bone structure that had previously been hidden by the heavy curtain of hair she invariably let fall over her face. 'And I like it.'

'Oh, *you* like it,' she drawled. 'That makes it all right then.'

Her acid sarcasm drew a smile from Theo.

Beth blinked and, heart beating too fast, lowered her eyelashes in a protective sweep. The smile softened the habitual hauteur of his expression, smoothing out some of the ingrained lines of cynicism bracketing his sternly sensual mouth; even she had to concede he was an incredible-looking man and when he smiled, like now... If he didn't have a girlfriend it was *definitely* out of choice, but the question in her mind still remained— 'Why?'

'Why?' Theo mused. She was posing a question he had asked himself on several occasions over the last three months. It was not from lack of opportunity. A man in his position would never lack offers of female companionship. This was an opinion formed more of cynicism than vanity. Women were attracted to position and power and he had no problem dating a woman who was more interested in what he represented than him.

In fact it suited him. He had no desire to be with a woman who *loved* him for himself, which would require that he gave more of himself than he had any desire to do.

Life was too short for the complications of emotional involvement and romantic love, if such a thing existed, was something he actively avoided, not aspired to.

Unconscious she had voiced the question for a second time until he echoed it, Beth stared at him blankly for a moment before lifting her chin. 'It's a fair question,' she lied defensively. 'You're the sort of man who has all the accessories—a flashy car, an expensive watch...' her eyes flickered to his wrist and she gave a smile; the watch was there, the dull metal gleaming against his dark skin '...and the obligatory blonde.'

Beth had to fight all the instincts that screamed retreat as Theo leaned towards her.

'Tonight I have a brunette.' He closed his eyes and inhaled.

'Mousey—' she corrected, adding, '—are you smelling my hair?'

'No, I'm smelling you.'

Was that meant to make her feel better?

Theo grinned into her astonished face and got out of the car, leaving her to achieve as dignified an exit as she could muster before he placed a wrap around her shoulders.

'You're on,' he whispered in her ear as he placed an arm around her waist.

Beth recognised the chef who emerged from the kitchen to greet Theo from the television. The two men spoke for a few minutes, drifting seamlessly from French, which Theo spoke fluently, to English before Theo drew her forward and introduced her.

The chef—apparently she was to call him Louis—kissed her hand with Gallic charm, saying some charming things that made Beth flush before he released her back to Theo.

'Your party are already here, I think, Theo?'

Theo received the information in stony silence; he had seen Louis's charm offensive before and found it amusing, but he discovered that it had lost some of its entertainment value for him.

Considering the French chef's reputation for showing diners who offended him the door—though, admittedly, it was hard to imagine anyone pulling that sort of stunt with Theo—Beth just hoped she had smiled in the right places because her nervous anticipation of the ordeal ahead had made it difficult for her to focus on what the famous man was saying.

She felt Theo's fingers tighten on her elbow as the maître d' confirmed their party was indeed already here. He was right to be worried; had it been an option, she would have been running in the opposite direction about now but she was operating on autopilot, capable of doing very little other than hyperventilate and move in the direction the guiding hand on her arm steered her.

The buzz of conversation in the restaurant softened to a soft hum as they entered. Theo barely registered the curious looks, at least the ones directed at him. 'So what do you think of Louis?'

Concentrating on putting one foot in front of the other, Beth searched for something to say. In truth, the man had made very little impression on her. 'He's nice...shorter than he looks on the television.'

'Don't take what he says too literally.' Theo warned as the maître d' led the way.

Even in her present state of abject gibbering terror, Beth registered the peculiar harshness in his voice. She angled a sideways glance at his face and found his expression correspondingly grim.

'You mean I'm not stunningly beautiful—imagine my shock,' she intoned drily.

His eyes narrowed in annoyance at her deliberate misinterpretation of his comment. 'I *mean* the man has a libido to match his ego and he has a reputation for...'

Astonished by the cold condemnation in his voice—since when did Theo Kyriakis become a member of the moral majority?—Beth gave a hoot of disbelief and cut across him. 'I thought the man was your friend, though I admit when it comes to egos you are the expert.'

'He is my friend, but that doesn't mean I would trust him with my sister.'

This piece of male logic drew a laugh of sheer disbelief from Beth. 'I'm not your sister.'

Theo looked at the top of her glossy head and realised that if his plan worked there was a strong possibility that one day she could be.

It was not a prospect that filled him with joy because the more he got to know this woman the more he realised that she would not suit his brother at all. Under normal circumstances his interest in Andreas's love life was minimal, but the more he saw of Elizabeth Farley the less he could see them suiting long-term. Maybe that was the problem—she was a long-term sort of female and also just about the most obstinate and opinionated woman he had ever met.

A thoughtful expression drifted across his face. It would be ironic if by solving one problem he might be creating another, but one problem at a time and right now saving his brother from Ariana's talons took priority.

The adrenaline rush generated by their heated, hissed interchange got her halfway across the large room, filled with well dressed diners, before the fear closed back in and her knees started to shake.

'You're doing great,' Theo murmured in her ear.

At one level amazed and on another a little disturbed that he was so intuitive to her feelings, Beth shivered, aware of the tingling sensation where his warm breath had brushed her skin.

'Either I'm paranoid or everyone is talking about us.' They were definitely looking—she could feel the critical pairs of eyes drilling into her back like knives.

'Let them talk; why should you care what these people say? You do not need their approval.'

Beth watched his dark eyes sweep dismissively across the heads of the diners and wished she had his genuine indifference. She doubted if he knew how rare it was. She was positive he didn't begin to understand most people's need for the good opinion of others.

'Why make their envy your problem?'

Responding to the pressure of the hand he placed in the small of her back, she walked a little ahead of him when the space between two tables made it impossible for them to walk side by side.

If she was in danger of forgetting just how arrogant and conceited Theo was, this comment acted as a timely reminder. 'So they envy me because I'm with you.'

His brows twitched into a straight line. 'They envy you because you are beautiful.'

There were a few other responses to her appearance washing around out there; it was not the first time that his female companion had attracted some lecherous stares, but it was the first time his female companion had been oblivious to the fact.

'Very funny.'

She flashed a resentful scowl up at his face and encountered an expression in Theo's compelling deep-set eyes that made her almost lose her footing.

Beth looked quickly away, her heart beating uncomfortably fast. 'I didn't know you had a sense of humour,' she muttered, concentrating on putting one foot in front of the other—anything but the hard predatory expression she had seen in his eyes.

'Relax, Elizabeth.'

Conscious that his eyes were watching the erratic rise and fall of her breasts, Theo struggled to follow his own advice. It seemed to him that every lecherous male in the room was similarly fixated.

Relax! Easy for him to say, she thought, sliding an aggrieved sideways glance at Theo's patrician profile. He had a lifetime's experience of people staring at him; he probably enjoyed being the centre of attention.

Though, actually, she mused, risking a second surreptitious glance at his lean face, Theo did not look the picture of cool; she thought, her glance sliding from the clenched angle of his jaw to the muscle throbbing in his cheek, he looked furious.

Before she could speculate further on the cause of his displeasure, the maître d' opened a door at the far end of the room and stood to one side while he waited for them to go through.

Beth held back, quivering from head to toe like a thoroughbred about to enter the slips.

To Theo, who had recently extended his interest in the equestrian world with the acquisition of a racehorse, the analogy seemed apt; she had the same innate elegance and grace of those highly strung, fascinating creatures.

'You look like you're going to the dentist. Smile, Elizabeth.'

'I *like* the dentist,' Beth hissed. She put up a moment's token resistance before responding to the light pressure on her shoulder. 'He is a charming man and I have excellent teeth,' she revealed, flashing the set in question at him in an insincere smile.

He didn't look at her as, pitching his voice to a low intimate rasp, he bent his head to hers. 'You have an excellent body also.'

Having successfully reduced her to angry blushing with the added bonus of pliant confusion, Theo casually looped an arm around her waist.

'What do you think you're doing?' Beth demanded, slapping at the hand that had slipped to the curve of her behind.

He gave a low husky chuckle and advised her to play nice, adding, 'Because you love me.'

A little choking cry emerged from her lips as he physically hauled her closer again. 'You love yourself.' He chuckled again, the low throaty sound making her stomach muscles quiver. 'I can't do this.'

'You are doing this,' he retorted. 'Now, is this so bad?' he asked as her curves somehow insinuated themselves snugly into the angles of his hard male body.

Beth found it alarming that her body seemed to be acting independently of her brain. 'But—'

He turned his head and pressed a finger to her parted

lips. 'Elizabeth, if you don't shut up I'll have to kiss you again.' His glance drifted to the full lush outline of her rosy lips and he found himself half hoping she would defy him.

Was that a threat or a promise? Beth wondered. Ever since it had happened, she had determinedly not thought about the moment his mouth had come down hard on her own. Now the mental barrier tumbled and it all came rushing back, the memory so clear, so detailed that it felt as though it was happening again.

She stared up at him, eyes half closed, pupils dilated as she relived the kiss in relentless detail. The smoky smouldering gleam in his densely lashed eyes as his head lowered, the fragrant warmth of his breath, the texture of his firm lips, the sensuous movement of his mouth and finally the erotic invasion of his tongue. In an attempt to delete the shameful memory of her enthusiastic response, Beth covered her eyes with her hand.

Theo slowly unpeeled her fingers one by one until he held her small hand between his own.

Their eyes held for a tense moment.

Beth broke the moment with a stiff little nod of assent. 'I'm ready.' For what? queried the voice in her head.

A slow grin spread across his lean features. 'Good girl.'

The verbal equivalent of a pat on the head. The patronising note of approval in his impossibly sexy voice made Beth grit her teeth and resort to sarcasm.

'I live to serve,' she gritted, averting her gaze from the disturbing gleam in his eyes.

'That's the spirit; just think sex slave and we're home and dry,' he murmured.

Beth knew that thinking it would be a mistake but she did anyway and the images that flashed through her mind threw her into a state of hot-cheeked confusion.

CHAPTER EIGHT

TAKING advantage of the moment, Theo bent his head and kissed her, a mere brushing of his lips against her own but it was enough to drive the last coherent thought from her mind and the strength from her knees.

While she was still blinking he led her into the room. Smaller than the main restaurant, this room was decorated in a similar art deco style, but Beth was oblivious to the décor, desperately conscious of the arm like a steel band that sealed her to his side in a lover-like embrace; she could only see the people seated around the table staring at her.

Convinced she might as well have *fake* emblazoned in neon along her forehead, she decided this moment had *graceful faint* written all over it. Though, as the moments of high anxiety in her life had not previously found release in graceful swoons but less graceful throwing up, the floor opening up and swallowing her would make a very acceptable substitute.

She tensed, waiting, fully anticipating that, any moment now, Andreas would indignantly demand to know what she was doing in that ridiculous get-up instead of double-checking those figures he needed on his desk by the morning.

But he didn't. When she glanced his way, Beth saw that he was staring at her, but with a total lack of recognition and also, she realised with a little flutter of shock, male appreciation.

Kissed and lusted after—being irresistible turned out to be quite unsettling.

Could it be this was actually going to work?

'Theo, you are late.'

Beth knew from the photo on Andreas's desk that the woman who reproached Theo was their mother, though, with her trim figure and smooth face, Daria Carides, as she was since her remarriage, looked too young to have grown sons.

Theo uncoiled his arm from around Beth's waist but retained her hand as he walked with her over to his mother and kissed the cheek she offered him.

'Sorry about that, Mother.' He glanced towards Beth and smiled, saying, 'We were...held up.'

The intimate smile suggested the hold-up had not involved a traffic jam but more carnal activities. Beth had no doubt that this had been his intention.

Theo met her reproachful glare with a grin that carried no regrets.

Daria watched the interplay, then looked her son up and down critically before pronouncing, 'You are too thin.'

Beth was glad of this small respite while the table's attention was momentarily diverted from her and amused to see Theo Kyriakis, who was spoken of in reverential terms in financial circles, a man feared and admired in equal measure, in the role of chastised meek son, though she couldn't totally agree with the maternal assessment.

Theo was, it was true, greyhound lean—the body she had recently been clamped to had not appeared to carry an ounce of excess flesh—but *thin* implied weak and scrawny; his tall athletic frame, all bone, sinew and muscle, was anything but weak. His every movement suggested a restrained power and strength.

Realising she was staring at him with what might appear to the casual observer to be longing, Beth lowered her gaze hurriedly.

Theo had to be used to the stares, though most were probably not as objective or clinical as her own, because even she recognised he did have a sexual charisma that was off the scale—all a bit too obvious and in-your-face for her, but Beth could see why there was never any shortage of candidates, eager to satisfy his healthy libido.

And his family were all meant to think she was one of them, that she was sleeping with him.

That was the role she had agreed to play. The important thing, she told herself as she suppressed a childish impulse to announce a denial to the room, was that she knew the truth— did it actually matter that these people looked at her and saw another notch in his bedpost?

Yes, it did!

She envied now, more than ever, Theo's complete indifference to the opinion of others.

Maybe she was just a prude?

She might even be frigid? Both were accusations that had been levelled at her by her last boyfriend. Did dinner and a trip to the cinema give the awful Clive boyfriend status? She had been totally taken in by his studious, unthreatening appearance—he had turned out to be a groper.

Beth knew she wasn't what people would call highly sexed but she didn't actually think she was prudish, though she accepted that being brought up by an elderly grandparent with very old-fashioned ideas had always set her apart from her contemporaries.

'You're like your father,' Daria sighed. 'You just burn

it off… You should slow down. And who is this, Theo?' Daria turned her attention to Beth.

In response to the question, Theo held out his free hand towards Beth, who reached out without thinking and found herself standing with both hands enfolded in a firm warm grip.

Tugging her towards him, Theo pulled her into his body and announced, 'This is Beth.' He stopped short of banging his chest, but the audible mixture of pride and possessiveness in his voice had much the same effect and made his mother look at Beth with increased interest.

Managing to tear her gaze from the warmth in Theo's eyes, Beth flashed a quick shy smile around the people sitting at the table.

'She can speak?' Daria asked lightly

Beth flashed him a look. 'When I can get a word in edgeways.'

At the sound of her low voice, Andreas, who had been staring at her with a puzzled expression, suddenly slapped the side of his head and exclaimed, 'It's my Beth!' He blinked in an almost dazed fashion as his gaze slid from the top of her head to her designer-shod feet as he half rose to his feet before subsiding back into his chair. 'What have you done to yourself?'

Noticing for the first time the attention his comments had drawn, he gave a sheepish shrug and said, 'Beth works for me.' His glance slid to his brother. 'I had no idea that you were…' Andreas's voice trailed away as once more his gaze made the journey from her toes to the top of her gleaming head. He swallowed hard and muttered something under his breath.

A woman? Beth thought, her lips twisting into a small wry smile as she recalled Theo's prediction that Andreas's eyes would pop out of his head—they were!

Mostly it was irritating when Theo was right but, on this occasion, she didn't mind. It was soothing to her ego to be noticed.

She was conscious she ought to be enjoying this moment of triumph more than she was but, for some bizarre reason, while the brother she had been crazy about for years was staring at her with open mouthed appreciation, all she was conscious of was the tall brooding presence of the other brother standing silently beside her.

'Beth, this is my mother and her husband, Georgios.' The thick-set man with grey-streaked hair and nice eyes smiled and got to his feet.

Daria Carides smiled warmly and said, 'Beth—what a charming name—come sit by me, dear.'

Beth found herself looking to Theo for guidance. He nodded imperceptibly and, after a pause, she took the empty chair beside his mother. It said a lot for her state of mind that she was relieved when Theo sat in the chair beside her.

The relief changed to something else when she felt his iron-hard thigh push close against her own. She felt no desire to examine this new feeling; instead, she shifted sideways in her seat to break the contact.

Georgios Carides said something in Greek to Theo as he retook his own seat. Beth knew from odd comments that Andreas had let slip that he had a problem with the man his mother had married soon after the death of her first husband.

Watching Theo's relaxed manner as he laughed in response to his stepfather's comment, it seemed that he did not share his brother's reservations about the older man.

'Andreas you know, and, of course—' Theo paused, his glance sweeping over the woman sitting beside Andreas, '—Ariana. You have met Beth?'

Ariana delivered a practised smile but the barely repressed fury glowing in her blue eyes as they swept across Beth's face sent a real bunny-boiler message.

Beth smiled back, determined not to let the other woman know how spooked she was.

Beth was far too practical to believe in premonitions of danger but she did not resist the protective arm that Theo placed around her shoulder. It was actually possible she might have leaned into him and it felt good when his thigh pressed once more into her own.

'So, Beth, my dear, how long have you two known one another?' Daria flashed her elder son a teasing look and asked, 'Was it love at first sight?'

'No, I thought he was the rudest, most arrogant man I had ever met.'

'And I thought she was a prudish prig.'

Andreas, who had listened to this exchange with a petulant frown, shook his head. 'Neither of you breathed a word; how long?'

'These things sometimes take no time at all.'

Under the table, Beth kicked his shin and said, 'So have you set a date?'

Having successfully diverted the conversation away from herself, Beth listened with half an ear to the discussion of spring weddings and designer wedding gowns. The starters had been removed and they were halfway through the main course and the conversation, dominated by Ariana, still revolved around weddings. Beth, who had not contributed to the discussion, jumped when directly asked her opinion by Daria.

Daria repeated her question. 'So what would your perfect wedding be, Beth?'

Beth, who started at the sound of her name, responded without considering her reply. 'I don't think it really matters what sort of wedding you have; it's what comes after that counts.'

'I thought all little girls dreamed of floating down the aisle,' Georgios teased.

'Well, I think that's kind of refreshing,' Andreas said, seemingly oblivious to the icy dagger glare his fiancée was giving him as he gave Beth a warm look. 'You know,' he mused, resting his chin on his steepled fingers, 'I just can't get over it; at work you look so different, and your hair, and—'

'Andreas—' his mother laughed '—the girl can hardly wear an evening dress to the office.'

'No, it's more than that. I just can't get over it.'

'I suggest you do.' The level look Theo flashed his brother made the younger man straighten up. 'There is no mystery,' Theo added as he reached out and covered the small hand that lay on the snowy tablecloth with his own. Beth started slightly and he applied warning pressure before he lifted her hand. 'Even today, some beautiful women think they have to hide their beauty to be taken seriously.' Pressing a kiss to her palm, he retained her hand.

Beth expected people to fall about laughing but instead they appeared to treat Theo's crazy comment seriously.

Andreas was staring at her like a man who'd just been hit over the head with something hard and heavy. 'Yes, she is…' He cleared his throat, lowered his gaze to his plate and added, 'I mean *you* are. Beautiful, that is, Beth.'

Beth was sure she would have enjoyed the moment a lot more had Ariana not been glaring at her in a way that made her want to request the knives on the table be removed. As it was, she felt inclined to ask Andreas why, if she was so beautiful, he had never noticed before.

'Surely it's not still that bad,' Daria said, permitting herself a discreet smile as her glance slid to the hand that Theo held pressed to his heart.

'How many times have you heard people say "I wonder who she slept with to get the job?"' her husband inserted.

'Well, I think it's a sad reflection on modern society,' Andreas said.

'Well, I've never had a problem being taken seriously,' his fiancée interjected.

'But not all women are as...confident as you are, Ariana,' her future mother-in-law observed quietly. She turned to Beth and asked, 'Have *you* never been tempted to trade on your looks, Beth?'

Beth pulled her hand from Theo's and tucked it safely in her lap. 'No, I haven't,' she was able to respond with total honesty. She didn't dare look at Ariana; she almost felt sorry for her—*almost*.

She smiled at the waiter who took away her plate and took a sip of her wine, losing control of the glass as she returned it to the table and spilling wine on the tablecloth.

Under cover of mopping up the spill with her napkin, she looked across at Andreas, who gazed back innocently, though his lips did twitch when her eyes widened.

CHAPTER NINE

BETH closed her eyes and let the cold water play over her wrists. She closed her eyes, letting her head fall. 'What am I doing?'

'My thought exactly.'

The sound of his deep voice above the water rushing in the washbasin made Beth start violently and she pulled out her hands, sending drops of water flying all over the mirror and the man she had spun around to face.

'What am *I* doing?' she spat. 'What are *you* doing?' She glanced over her shoulder and was relieved to see all the stalls were empty. 'This, in case you didn't notice, is the Ladies room.' She fixed him with an accusing glare. 'Are you following me?'

'Clearly I am following you,' Theo said, brushing the water drops from his tie with an attitude of irritation.

'Why?'

'I thought you might have got lost.'

She rolled her eyes at the blatant lie. 'You thought I might have run away.'

He conceded the accusation with a shrug. 'I thought it was possible; you left the table looking...flustered.'

Beth's eyes fell from his.

'Did someone say something to you?' While he had

monitored the conversation as much as he could, it was not possible to screen everything that was being said.

Beth pursed her lips and shook her head. 'No.' She turned her back on him and began to replace the items she had removed from her bag to find her tissues—before she remembered that the tissues were one of the things she had no room for.

Theo strolled across the room and leaned an elbow on the marble counter where Beth was messing with her bag.

The silence stretched as she ignored him, which was not easy when she could literally feel his eyes on her face. Finally unable to bear it any longer, she flung down a lipstick in disgust and spun around to face him.

'What?'

His shrewd gaze swept her face. When it came to subterfuge, Elizabeth Farley was not skilled.

'Nobody said anything, but something did upset you and do not bother denying it,' he added as she opened her mouth. 'I have been lied to by experts and you are not an expert. I know four-year-olds who lie better than you; you are as transparent as glass.' In the survival stakes, this put her at an immediate disadvantage.

She flashed him a look of withering contempt and pushed her hands into the automatic drier, even though they had already dried. 'You make that sound like a bad thing,' she yelled above the noise of the violently efficient machine. 'Not *everyone* considers the inability to lie a failing, you know.'

His mouth curved in a triumphant smile. 'So you admit you are lying.'

She gritted her teeth in sheer exasperation, longing to wipe the smug smile off his face. 'I didn't know going to the Ladies room was a reason for interrogation. Did you bring your thumbscrews?' Not that he needed them; not when he had a stare that seemed to be able to see right into her head. An illusion, obviously, but one that made her feel distinctly uncomfortable.

'And what,' she added, unable to repress the urge that made her glance nervously over her shoulder, 'if anyone saw you come in here?'

Theo looked utterly unconcerned by the possibility. 'They will think, I imagine, that I felt the need to be alone with you.'

Beth blinked in confusion. 'Why would you need to be alone with me?'

He raised a brow and looked amused. 'Why do men normally wish to be alone with a beautiful woman?' There was a dark glitter in his heavy-lidded eyes as they came to rest on her lips that made Beth's stomach muscles quiver.

The penny dropped and Beth's face was suffused in an instant rosy blush. 'You're disgusting!' she choked, turning back to her handbag as though it was a safety blanket. Concentrating on the task in hand, she waited for the quivering in her belly to still.

'And you, Elizabeth, were trying to change the subject.'

His voice, deep and smooth as bitter chocolate, was far too close. Beth stopped trying to shovel the contents of her bag back in—strangely, they no longer fitted—and, flicking a strand of hair from her eyes, snarled, 'That is the subject.'

'No, you leaving the table looking like a startled rabbit is the subject. What happened to throw you into a total panic? I will know!' he told her sternly.

Their eyes clashed and, as she studied his face, she saw the relentless determination in those powerfully carved lines and she felt her resolve crumble.

She believed him.

Theo did not say things for effect; he did not bluff. He was a man who would always follow through with a threat or a promise.

Beth exhaled and threw up her hands in an attitude of weary defeat. 'All right, you want to know—fine.'

Theo narrowed his eyes and prompted, 'Well?'

'If you must know, Andreas…he…I thought it was the table leg and then…he stroked my leg with his foot.'

Theo's hands clenched at his sides, but his voice was bland as he said, 'My brother played footsie with you at the table?' Andreas was nothing if not predictable.

Beth nodded.

'And you ran away?'

'What did you expect me to do—play footsie back?' she demanded indigantly.

'Well, wasn't that the idea? Haven't you been wanting him to make a move on you for three years?'

And when it came she had not felt the way she had imagined. 'But he's engaged.' That had to be why she hadn't felt excited but actually dismayed.

'Temporarily.'

'And she was sitting there and you were sitting there and…it would be like…' Her voice lowered to a whisper as she added guiltily, 'Cheating.'

'I hate to tell you this, but we are not actually an item so you would not technically be cheating.'

'Andreas doesn't know that.'

'You are not being rational.'

Beth glared at him, opened her mouth to deny the claim and discovered she couldn't. There was nothing that even approached *rational* in the jumble of emotions spinning around in her head. With a grunt of frustration, she turned away but, before she could thrust her hands into the drier again, Theo captured them and spun her back to him.

She tugged angrily but he held her fast, his brown fingers curled around her wrists. She raised her angry eyes to his face and after a few moments stopped struggling.

'That thing,' he observed, slinging a censorious glance at the offending item, 'makes more noise than a jet landing and your hands are dry.' To prove the point he turned them over, his thumbs running slowly across her palms.

A strange inertia washed over Beth as she watched him trace a slow arabesque over her skin, the light contact sending needles of sensation scudding along her nerve endings.

She shivered as she experienced the weirdest impulse to lean into him.

Theo released her and, placing a finger under her chin, tilted her face up to him.

'I never expected it to actually work,' she admitted in response to the question in his eyes. 'But I suppose you're right. He does want what you have, or,' she added hastily, 'what he thinks you have. I didn't think that Andreas was like that.'

'My brother changes his women as frequently as he changes his socks.'

'I know, but he wasn't engaged before.'

'You have discovered your idol has feet of clay. So you no longer love him because he does not live up to your high standards?'

'Of course I love him.' Hearing the uncertainty in her own voice, Beth added, more firmly, 'Of course I do.'

'Then you should be happy that things are going so well.'

The shrewd expression in his eyes as he studied her face made Beth feel uncomfortable. Her lips twisted into a grimace. 'You make it sound so cold-blooded and...I don't want to trap Andreas.'

His lips curled. 'It's what women have been doing for centuries.'

Her angry eyes were spitting sparks as they flew to his lean face. 'If I was as cynical as you I'd—'

Theo cut across her. 'It's not going to happen.' His eyes narrowed as he studied her angry face. She was a peculiar combination of spiky aggression and impractical starry-eyed idealism.

'You have made Andreas a white knight in your dreams. He is not—no man is. The question is, do you want a man or a fantasy?'

She made a negative motion with her head, the action causing her silky hair to whip wildly about her face.

Theo caught her chin in his hand and studied her soft features. An abstracted expression drifted across his face as he lifted his hand to brush a shiny strand of hair from her cheek.

The glow in his eyes was hypnotic. Beth's chest tightened as the emotions locked inside swelled. She was close enough to him to feel the warmth of his body. This close, the aura of raw masculinity he projected was strong enough to make her dizzy. She exhaled a shaky breath and closed her eyes momentarily as she fought for composure, as her nostrils quivered in response to the slightly citrus scent of the fragrance he used, overlaid with musky warm male.

She had been in love with Andreas for three years and during that time she had frequently worked in close physical proximity with him. And, even though Andreas was quite a tactile person, it had never been a problem for her. Sex, or the lack of it, had never got in the way.

Theo was someone she didn't even like, let alone love, and yet bizarrely she had never been aware of Andreas as a man, not this way. She couldn't even concentrate in the same room as Theo.

He felt the shiver run through her body as his finger grazed her cheek. Their glances locked, stormy green on predatory black.

'I'm not on trial here.' Beth had to force the words past the ache in her throat.

Theo felt the moment the heat generated by their mutual antipathy morphed into something else, different but still hot.

Beth was the first to look away. 'It's warm in here.'

Now this, he thought, breathing through the primal urge to crush her mouth under his, was not something that he had calculated for, but it should not be a problem. A little genuine chemistry might even help the cause as long as he did not lose focus…but focus had never been a problem for him.

Theo straightened and was about to move away—focus, on this occasion, might work better with some breathing space—when a slight movement in the periphery of his vision alerted him to the fact they were not alone.

His nostrils flared as he caught a whiff of the heavy exotic perfume that Ariana, not a big believer in the maxim *less is more*, doused herself with.

Changing direction, he stepped into Beth and spanned her waist with his big hands.

Beth's head came up with a snap, her eyes widening in shock. 'What do you—?' Her voice trailed away, the expression of dark intent etched into the strong lines of his lean face freezing her to the spot.

He picked her up and sat her on the marble counter.

'I want you.'

The raw statement drove every coherent thought from her head. She shook her head, aware of the thunderous roar in her ears and the bright lights dancing before her eyes. She felt dizzy and breathless with anticipation.

She stilled, not breathing, as Theo lowered his head and she thought, *He's going to kiss me...again. I want him to kiss me again!*

Beth's eyes widened at the shocking realisation and then closed tight as he fitted his mouth to hers. She rose in his arms, her legs shifting to either side of his rock-hard thighs as she pressed her body to his, winding her arms around his neck as she opened her mouth willingly to the carnal invasion of his tongue.

Each successive stabbing incursion into the warm interior of his mouth made the muscles low in her pelvis tighten and twist—she wanted the feeling of both pleasure and pain to go on for ever; she wanted this kiss to go on for ever.

She was in his arms, soft and pliant, making little choking sounds in her throat that drove him crazy when the sexual tension that Theo had felt between them all day suddenly exploded, his mind went blank and he forgot why he was kissing her—he was just kissing her because it felt good and it felt right.

Beth twisted in his arms and felt his hands slide down the curve of her spine.

She moaned as he nipped at the soft flesh of her full swollen lips, catching the sensitive flesh in his teeth and tugging softly. She felt his hand curve over her breast and she breathed, 'Yes,' against his mouth and kissed him back—hard.

The carnal hunger coursing like fire through her veins leapt higher as she pressed her hands to the hard muscled ridges of his flat belly. He sucked in a breath and groaned, the cry wrenched from deep in his chest.

'I'm sorry to interrupt.'

Beth opened her eyes, trying to drag herself clear of the sensual thrall that still fogged her senses.

She blinked as she saw Ariana standing in the doorway.

The woman gave a hard little smile and turned, letting the heavy door swing closed behind her.

His eyes on the now empty doorway, Theo gave a nod of satisfaction. 'I think she saw enough.'

'You knew she was there.' She stopped and wished the stupid question unsaid; it had hardly been a spontaneous expression of uncontrollable lust, it had all been a show for the other woman's benefit.

She wanted to cry, but pride stopped her.

His dark eyes were intent on her face as he asked, 'Didn't you?'

'Not at first; I thought you'd just lost your mind,' she told him, adopting an attitude of fake candour—*and he thought she couldn't lie*! 'But she wears a very distinctive perfume.'

It hung in the air now like an exotic cloud. Beth couldn't believe she hadn't noticed it. She had been too busy noticing other things. In an agony of mortified shame, she watched him tuck his shirt back into his trousers.

She had definitely not been a passive partner in that kiss; the heat that had been generated still lay coiled low in her pelvis.

'I prefer yours; it is more subtle.' The light flowery scent was still in his nostrils. His eyes slid to her mouth and the knot of frustration in his belly made its painful presence known.

He had reacted instinctively when he saw Ariana, but he had very quickly lost sight of the purely practical purpose.

'I don't wear perf—' She stiffened as he placed his hands around her waist.

'Relax,' he recommended, flashing a grin before he lifted her down from the counter. He did not immediately release her. Instead, he stood, his body curved over her, his hands still spanning her waist.

Her physical reaction to this man was terrifying. So much for not being a fan of the dark brooding type!

'You'll crease my dress.'

Their eyes met and for a split second she thought Theo was going to ignore her, then he inclined his head and released her.

An awful thought occurred to Beth. 'What if she...tells anyone what she saw?'

'I'm relying on it; I have total faith in Ariana's instinct to dish the dirt.' Ariana's voice drifted through Theo's head, spiteful and vindictive. Beth had no defences against a woman like that.

Or against a man like me?

He tightened his jaw and closed down the conscience-pricking inner dialogue.

Beth grimaced in distaste and moaned, 'I feel sick.'

'You are ill?'

She flashed him a look of intense irritation. 'No, I'm not ill.' But possibly insane; nothing else explained what she had just done. If Ariana had not spoken, bringing her back to earth, what would have happened?

Beth shook her head, unable to complete the thought.

'Then what is wrong?'

Beth glared up at him. 'Beyond the fact I feel cheap and soiled after being mauled by you?' The moment the words left her lips, she knew that bringing up the subject had not been a good move.

One corner of his fascinating mouth twisted into a mocking half smile, though it was not mockery that put the heat in his stare.

'You did your fair share of mauling.' He thought of her

small cool hands moving over his skin and cleared his throat before tucking his already tucked shirt back into his trousers again.

The mortified colour rushed to her cheeks, her eyes locking of their own accord onto his mouth.

She tried not to remember the taste of him, the warm texture, the…Beth inhaled and pushed away the intrusive memories, wrapping her arms around herself to disguise the fact she was shaking.

It was hard to occupy the moral high ground when you'd just acted like a sex-starved bimbo, she thought, watching him casually straighten his tie, unable to believe that he could kiss like that and then act as though nothing had happened.

'You know I felt sorry for Ariana at dinner.'

Theo looked at her in utter disbelief. 'You don't have the survival skills of a lemming; you'll leap to your doom thinking the best of the world.'

Beth blinked at this blast of searing anger—where had that come from?

Taking a deep breath, she struggled to kick-start her frozen brain. His anger was baffling, his mouth was utterly distracting; the sensually sculpted outline acted as an irresistible lure.

'Do you want Andreas to marry a cold, manipulative bitch?'

Beth gave a contemptuous sniff. 'I'm sure you could teach her a thing or two about being cold and manipulative.' She thought about the searing heat of his kiss and added in a shaking voice, 'You can't have her so you don't want your brother to have her.'

His jaw tightened in anger, but Theo shrugged and let

the accusation stand. She clearly found it easier to assign base motives to his actions, and her liking him was not essential to the success of this scheme.

And kissing her was not essential either but it had been pleasurable, as his body was still reminding him. The physical and sexual had always been something that he was able to control.

Theo held open the door for her to pass through, but Beth hesitated.

'What's wrong now?' he asked, sounding like a man very near the limit of his patience.

'If you must know, the idea of walking back in there with people thinking what they're thinking...' She gave an expressive shudder.

His lips twisted into a sardonic smile. 'And what would that be?'

She flashed him a look of dislike. 'That I'm the sort of girl who—' She stopped and bit her lip.

Theo laughed. 'If by "people" you mean Andreas, don't worry; that's the sort of girl he likes.'

'And what sort of girl do you like? My God!' she groaned. 'I said that out loud, didn't I?'

The dismayed addition thawed some of the tension in the atmosphere as Theo grinned. The unexpected warmth in his expression made her stare. Once she started, it was hard to stop—there was something about his dark fallen angel face that made it compulsive viewing.

'I like variety, Elizabeth.'

'You mean you're not fussy. Personally, I prefer quality to quantity.' Quite pleased she'd given the impression she was not only discriminating but something of an expert on the subject, Beth wrinkled her nose and gave a disdainful sniff.

'While I find details of your sex life fascinating—' despite the mockery in his tone, he recognised there was an underlying truth in his comment '—I think we should join the party before they send out another search party.' Or I kiss you again.

'Fine by me,' Beth snapped, hurrying to keep pace with his long-legged stride, her progress hampered by the long skirt of her dress and the unaccustomed height of her heels.

Theo paused and waited, hands folded across his chest for her to catch up. 'Don't dawdle.'

'You try hurrying in a dress that has built-in wind resistance.'

His lips twitched. 'I'll pass.'

'And heels,' she continued to grumble, extending one leg and pointing to her toes to demonstrate her point. 'And, in case you hadn't noticed, I don't have legs that go all the way up to my ears!'

But they were very nice legs—actually, better than nice—and, from what he'd seen, perfectly in proportion with the rest of her diminutive frame.

Theo's glance moved from her slender ankle and up over her equally shapely calf. In his head, he saw his fingers pushing aside the black fabric and sliding underneath higher and higher until he reached the damp heat of… He stopped and lifted his gaze abruptly.

This was what happened when a man neglected a healthy libido; it was *definitely* time to find a replacement for Camilla.

'You want me to say you have great legs? Fine, I will. You have great legs,' he said, sounding bored.

'The day I need your approval is the day I have myself sectioned.' Head held high, skirt in hand, she stalked past him, inadvertently providing him with an excellent view of her rear.

Stopping short of re-entering the dining room, Beth stopped. 'We can't go back in together.'

'Let me guess.' Theo rolled his eyes. 'What will people think?'

CHAPTER TEN

DESPITE his mockery, Theo had agreed without much of an argument to leave a decent interval before he returned to the table.

He didn't seem to understand her embarrassment but then why would a man who had the sensitivity of a rhinoceros appreciate her discomfiture?

To Beth's relief, there were no sly comments made about their prolonged absence from the table. Theo dropped the attentive lover routine, which was a massive relief. In fact he ignored her so completely that she got the impression that people thought they'd had a row.

She might actually have enjoyed the rest of the meal but for Ariana's icy glares and Andreas's tendency to stare.

They were lingering over coffee when Beth's phone beeped.

'Sorry.' Beth flashed a smile round the table and fished her phone from the impracticably tiny bag that matched her outfit.

When she had voiced her concern about its size, the stylists, clearly shocked by her ignorance, had exchanged glances before mentioning the designer of the tiny beaded handbag with what seemed to Beth inappropriate reverence.

Theo watched the expressions flicker across her face as

she read the text and wondered who or what had put the fear in her eyes.

With a mild jolt of shock he realised that he knew nothing about her personal life.

He had no idea about her family or friends; he didn't know if she liked Chinese food or Italian. This information, he realized, could be useful when it came to presenting the image of a loving couple.

It was Andreas who spoke first when she slid the phone away. 'Problem with the contracts?' he asked. 'Their accountant had no problem with the figures when I ran them past him so there shouldn't be.'

Beth shook her head and cut across him. 'No, it's not work; it's personal.'

'Personal?' Andreas echoed.

'Yes,' she snapped and saw his eyes widen at the unaccustomed brusqueness in her tone. She had had enough of the Kyriakis brothers tonight. 'I do have a life outside the office.' Another time the hurt expression that chased across Andreas's good-looking face might have made her feel guilty but right now her thoughts were focused on the news from the nursing home.

She smiled an apology around the table, leaving Theo until last. She did not expect him to be pleased at her leaving before the evening had ended after all the trouble and expense he had gone to but if he didn't like it, she thought grimly—tough.

'I'm afraid I have to leave; my gran is not very well.' The doctors had warned after the last episode that the likelihood was there would be more.

That had been eight months ago and, when gran had not suffered any long-term damage from the minor stroke, the fear Beth had felt at the time had receded.

'Nothing serious, I hope?' Daria asked.

Theo watched her knead her white fingers, tying them into knots as she gave a tight little smile, her thoughts clearly already elsewhere.

'They say not, but—'

Andreas looked flatteringly eager when he cut across her and said, 'Well, in that case, there's no hurry, is there? Why break up the party?' he coaxed, oblivious to the molten fury in Ariana's glare before she lowered her gaze to her plate.

'I'm sorry, but—'

'Of course she has to go, Andreas.' Theo slung a look of irritation in his brother's direction.

Beth watched in utter amazement as Theo laid down his napkin and got his feet. She watched, her mouth slightly ajar, as he kissed his mother's cheek, saying something soft to her in his native tongue before he took a position behind her own chair.

Feeling wary but grateful that he was not making this difficult for her, at least here, she got to her feet.

Georgios stood up and, after a speaking glance from his mother, so did Andreas.

'We hope your grandmother is better very soon,' Daria said, kissing her cheek. 'And, if you are able, we would love to see you next month Theo?'

Distracted, Beth only listened with half an ear as Theo agreed to the invitation on her behalf. Plenty of time later to say she had not signed up for family weekends.

She did not speak until they were outside in the street, then she held out her hand and said, 'I'm sorry about this.'

His hooded gaze slid to the hand extended to him but he did not take it. 'You are sorry for what?'

'Well, I've spoiled your plans,' she said, letting her hand fall to her side. Presumably, now that they were out of sight of his target audience, he would drop the act, which was good because even fingertip contact with him was slightly disturbing.

'I am presuming you did not arrange for your grandmother to be ill?'

Her eyes flew wide with indignation. 'Of course not!'

His broad shoulders lifted in an expressive shrug. 'Then there is very little more to be said. Some things in life one has no control over.' Fortunately, the sexual frustration he had been denying all evening—you couldn't rise above something until you acknowledged it—was not one of them.

'Well, thanks,' she said awkwardly as she watched a cab approach the taxi rank opposite. 'I'm sorry it didn't work out but I...' Anxious to be gone, worry lying like a weight in her chest, she shook her head. 'I'll...' She stepped towards the kerb.

'What are you doing?' It had started to rain fine drops that clung to her eyelashes as she tilted her head back to look at him.

Beth looked down at the fingers curled around her elbow. 'Catching a taxi.'

'Don't be stupid; I'll take you.'

Beth stared at him. 'You don't even know where I'm going.'

'I will when you tell me,' he countered smoothly.

Beth weighed her choices. She did not want to travel with Theo but there was no question that he would get her there faster than a taxi. It was the realisation that there hadn't been room for her purse in the ridiculous bag she was carrying that swung her decision.

'All right...thanks.'

In the underground garage, Theo told the driver they would not be needing his services before opening the passenger door for Beth. Belted into the passenger seat, Beth gave him the directions to the home.

'Do you want me to pick anyone else up on the way there? Your parents?'

Beth turned her head. 'No, they died—a train crash—I was seven so I don't really remember it.'

She just remembered waking up in the hospital and crying from the pain of the burns on her feet. She'd been there for weeks and Gran had stayed the entire time, sleeping in a cot at her bedside.

'You have no family?'

Beth bit her quivering lip and turned her head so that he wouldn't see the tears in her eyes. 'Just me and Gran. She brought me up after the accident.'

She was glad that Theo did not ask any more questions. Other than giving him directions, neither did Beth. Her thoughts were elsewhere, trying to imagine her life without her grandmother in it—she couldn't.

At the nursing home Beth was greeted warmly by the manager. 'The doctor's with your grandmother now.'

Fearful to ask the question and even more fearful of the reply, Beth said, 'How is she? Do you think she'll have to go to hospital again?' Seeing her grandmother looking so small and frail lying in the hospital bed had been the moment that Beth had been forced to face the fact that the indomitable lady would not be with her for ever.

He shook his head and looked sympathetic. 'We don't know yet, but Prudence is a tough lady. Let me take you up.' He directed an enquiring look at Theo, who stood, a silent observer to the interchange. 'Would you both like to see her?'

Beth shook her head and said quickly, 'No, this is just a friend who gave me a lift.' She turned, her luminous eyes brushing his face as she said, 'Thank you.'

Choosing not to analyse either the tenderness that moved though him as he watched her climb the flight of stairs or the stab of dissatisfaction he had experienced when she had called him *just a friend*, Theo lowered himself into a seat and prepared to wait.

Whatever the news, he thought, she would need *a friend* when she returned.

It was half an hour later that Theo saw the small figure at the top of the stairs. The harsh electric light overhead shone on her glossy head and revealed the wetness on her cheeks.

He put down the mug in his hands and got to his feet. 'I'm sorry.'

Beth reached the bottom of the stairs and stopped at the sound of his voice. 'No...no.' She dragged her hand across her wet cheeks and shook her head. 'No, I'm not crying... well, I am,' she admitted with a sniff. 'But not because— Gran is fine.' She gave a sunny smile, oblivious to the sharp intake of breath it drew from Theo. 'It's just the relief.'

'I'm glad your grandmother is well.'

She produced another smile that lit up her entire face.

Beth gave a puzzled frown. 'You waited.' The oddness of him still being here struck her for the first time. 'I thought you'd gone.'

'I thought you might need...'

'A shoulder to cry on?' She stopped, the smile sliding off her face as she added quickly, 'Not seriously?'

She'd realised about ten seconds after meeting him that Theo Kyriakis was more the pull-yourself-together sort of man, though, when it came to shoulders, his were certainly broad enough.

'I thought you might need transport.'

On anyone else, she would have called his manner

embarrassed. Was he afraid that a kind gesture might ruin his reputation?

'There was really no need for you to stay.'

He shrugged. 'I have not wasted the time. I caught up on some calls without interruption and, as you see, I have been well looked after.' He glanced to the mug and plate of untouched—Theo did not have a sweet tooth—biscuits on the table.

'I'm glad someone brought you tea.'

'Actually, I am not quite sure what it is.'

The comment drew a laugh from Beth, who was still feeling light-headed with relief and inclined to see the best in everyone, even Theo.

Her laughter was a stark contrast to the silent distress he had been conscious of on the journey here. 'So would you like a lift home?'

Beth regarded him doubtfully, unable to tell from his oddly abrupt manner if the offer was sincere or not. 'I wouldn't like to put you to any trouble.'

His brows lifted. 'Would you like a lift?' he repeated.

The flash of irritation in his eyes made Beth relax slightly. Theo being polite just didn't feel right. She tipped her head in a tiny nod of assent and said, 'I'd be grateful.'

On another occasion, Theo might have been tempted to ask *how grateful* but he suppressed his ignoble instincts and escorted her back to the waiting car.

Behind the driving wheel, he paused expectantly.

Beth shook her head in response to his questioning glance.

'Your address?'

Beth gave a self-conscious grimace. 'Of course. Sorry, I didn't think.'

Theo was surprised when Beth gave him the necessary information. The address she supplied was that of an extremely upmarket area, the home of bankers, City types and a high proportion of wealthy foreigners who had been drawn by the good transport links into the City, excellent schools and above average share of green spaces.

He was not in the habit of pigeonholing people but Beth did not act the way he would have expected someone who came from an affluent background to behave.

As he drew up in the tree-lined avenue outside the big double gates of the address she had given, the inconsistency was solved.

The house was the largest by far in the affluent street but it was also in a sadly neglected condition—actually, neglected was generous; it looked derelict. The place was a speculator's dream and worth a small fortune.

Beth saw him staring at the house and said defensively, 'The west wing is perfectly habitable. Though the roof in the east wing is pretty much shot,' she admitted with a sigh. The quote she had got last year to fix it had been laughable.

'That is a lot of house,' Theo observed diplomatically.

A wistful expression drifted across her face. 'I've seen pictures of it when Gran came here after she was married. It was quite grand and really beautiful; they still had servants then and the grounds were so pretty... There are still lots of daffodils in the spring.' Sadly, the rest of the original landscaping had been overgrown for years.

'You live here alone?' It was hard to imagine a place less suitable for a young woman to live.

'Until Gran comes home.'

The defensive prickles were back; he was guessing that this had been a point of dissension. 'Your grandmother does not live in the nursing home on a permanent basis?'

She sent him a challenging glare. 'No, she's coming home.'

'But until then you are alone?'

Beth nodded and opened the passenger door. 'That's the way I like it.'

Theo let the rather obvious lie pass. 'I'll see you inside.'

Beth shook her head vigorously. 'No, I'll be fine.'

Before he could respond, she fled. Theo waited in the car until a light went on inside and waited some more before he finally drove away. It seemed rather symbolic to him that one half of the rusting gate fell off its hinges as he did so.

CHAPTER ELEVEN

THEO walked into the office, his eyes automatically going to the desk in the corner.

It was empty.

Frowning, he walked to the closed door of his brother's office and walked in without warning.

A man did not value something that came easily. And for some men the pursuit was an important part of the mating ritual—his brother was definitely such a man.

How many times had he heard him say *easy come, easy go*?

This was not something he would have needed to explain to a normal female but he had realised last night when sleep had not come as easily as it normally did that Beth was not a normal female, she lacked all the normal female instincts.

Had he left it too late to explain this?

Had she kissed his brother the way she had kissed him last night? He was sure that if she had, his brother would not display similar restraint.

He had convinced himself that he would walk in on a scene of seduction.

The scene inside stopped him in his tracks, but it was not a scene of seduction but one of devastation.

His brother's desk was piled high with open files, papers had spilled out on to the floor and Andreas, swivelling in his chair from one side to the other, was swearing fluently through clenched teeth as he sifted through the papers spread out in a swathe across the desk.

In response to the dramatic release of tension, Theo began to laugh.

Andreas looked up, his expression indignant. 'You think this is funny?'

Theo lifted his brows in response. 'There is a problem?'

'You think…? Some idiot,' Andreas gritted, 'digging a hole in the street has cut through a power cable.'

'I did see some activity outside,' Theo admitted.

His brother shook his head in disbelief. 'And I thought you were the super-observant one. Some activity…? There are about a dozen trucks out there.'

'I had other things on my mind.' Like you making love to your assistant on the desk, which could not happen yet.

'Is this another example of love turning a cunning business brain to mush?' When Theo did not respond, he added, 'You must have noticed there are no lifts?'

'I don't use lifts. I walk up the stairs.' Theo angled a speculative look at the younger man's middle and added, 'A practice you might like to take up.'

Finding Theo's relentless good humour wearing, Andreas scowled. 'That will happen about the same time I take up hiking in the wilderness for pleasure and not shaving for a week. Unlike you, I do not see the attraction of unnecessary exercise, nature or simpler times. I like pavements, lifts and computers…especially,' he added with feeling, 'computers. I need those figures!' He narrowed his eyes. 'Are you laughing?'

Theo adopted a sober expression. 'Sorry, but it was the novelty value of seeing you breaking a sweat at work.'

'Yes, we all know you lead by example and never ask anyone to do anything you can't do yourself, but others among us believe in delegation and surrounding ourselves with the best people.'

'Talking of the best people, where is Elizabeth?'

'If you mean *Beth*, I've not the faintest idea. She didn't turn up this morning. I assumed you were the reason. Now where…?'

Theo planted both hands on the desk and leaned forward towards his brother. 'Beth did not come into work?'

'No, and I don't mind telling you it couldn't come at a worse time. She's never even had a day off before.'

Theo felt a flash of anxiety. 'She did not ring in or leave a message?'

'No.'

Theo regarded his brother, who sat there looking totally unconcerned, with an expression of sheer disbelief. 'And it did not occur to you that there might be something wrong?'

Andreas, startled by the repressed violence in his brother's manner, held up his hands in a pacifying gesture. 'No, as I said, I assumed she was with you.' A speculative light entered his eyes as he studied his brother's rigid face and asked hopefully, 'Have you two had a fight?'

Theo picked a file from the desk, handed it to his brother and said, 'This is the one you need.'

'Now, how,' Andreas wondered out loud, 'did you know that?'

He was talking to thin air. Theo was gone.

When Theo drew up outside the house there was already a car parked in the driveway. The place looked even worse in daylight. The crumbling grandeur and decay would not, he was sure, meet with the approval of the upmarket residents of the area.

He was walking up the path when the door opened and two men walked out. Even if their suits and manner had not proclaimed their profession, the expression on Beth's face would have.

The eyes, big and tragic, said it all.

Emotions he barely recognised swelled inside his chest. She was pale as a ghost, the vacant emptiness in her eyes emphasised by the smudges of dark colour beneath them.

There was a delay of seconds before he saw the recognition flash into her eyes. She lifted her hand in a fluttery gesture, then she looked at it as though she had forgotten why it was there and let it fall away.

'I'm fine,' she said before Theo could say anything.

Should she know why Theo was here? She considered the question with the same strange detached calm that she had been feeling ever since they had rung early that morning to break the news that her gran had passed away peacefully in her sleep.

'I'm sorry. Was I meant to—?' Her voice trailed away as though she had forgotten what to say.

Theo put his hands on her shoulders gently and turned her around. She walked ahead of him into the house.

The musty damp smell hit him immediately. 'Where's the kitchen?'

Beth looked at him vaguely and pointed to the far end of the hallway.

She sat and watched him move around the kitchen, filling the kettle, opening and closing cupboards and drawers. On one level she knew he ought not to be here but she couldn't work up the enthusiasm to tell him to go away.

Theo dropped into a squatting position by the chair she sat in.

'Drink it,' he said, closing her fingers around the mug.

Beth shook her head but he was insistent. She grimaced as she swallowed.

'I don't take sugar.'

'Today you do; it's for shock.'

He waited until she had drained the cup and then pulled out one of the other chairs and sat down.

'Your grandmother is gone?'

Gone sounded so permanent and it was. Beth could almost hear the sound as the ice around her heart cracked. Like frozen extremities when the circulation returned, the pain was take-your-breath-away burningly intense.

She would never see her gran again.

She bit her lip hard and nodded. Theo's dark eyes held compassion and sadness as though he knew what she was feeling.

Maybe he did—maybe he had lost someone he cared for too. A memory surfaced. He had lost a brother.

'They took Gran her cup of tea this morning and she didn't wake up.' She tried to put the cup down but her hands were shaking so hard she kept missing the table.

'I'm very sorry, Beth,' Theo said quietly. Her sadness was so profound he could feel it like a physical presence.

He knew that later she would resent him for seeing her this way—vulnerable—because this was not the face that Beth liked to present to the world, but he was nevertheless glad he was here for her.

She should not be alone right now—no one should at such a time—but, while he wanted to help, he didn't have the faintest idea how. Anything he could say seemed hopelessly inadequate.

'Let me.' He took the cup from her and set it on the table.

She reached out, her cold fingers closing over his hand as she said, 'I was thinking,' she began eagerly. 'It *can't* be right. Yesterday, they said she was fine; the doctor said she was fine. Do you think it might be a mistake?'

Theo shook his head slowly. He had to quash the hope in her eyes but he did it as gently as he could, which actually was not very gentle, the situation was by its very nature brutal.

'They didn't make a mistake, Beth, you know this.'

A small sound escaped her pale lips and the first tear slipped down her cheek. He reached out and dabbed it with the pad of his thumb.

Beth nodded as the tear was joined by another and another. 'She just went to sleep, they said,' she told him thickly. 'There was no pain.'

'That's good.'

Her head fell forward and Theo watched her narrow shoulders heaving as her slender frame was racked by silent sobs.

He watched for a few moments, struggling with a massive sense of helplessness. Then, with a rough word of comfort, he placed a hand at the back of her head and pulled it into his chest.

Beth gave a sob into his shirt.

The lost sound made Theo stiffen. He felt like a man who had seen a blow coming but had ducked too late. He looked down at the glossy head pressed against his heart, wincing every time she released another heartbreaking sob. She held onto him, her arms wrapped around his middle like someone who had been treading water too long and needed someone else to take the weight.

Theo stroked her hair back in long sweeping motions

and said soothing things. It didn't seem to matter that they were in his own tongue and eventually the outburst of raw emotion reduced.

Her sobs became intermittent hiccoughs.

He felt the moment her control returned.

She lifted her face, cast a slightly embarrassed look up at him and pulled away, wiping her face with the heels of her hands. 'I have things I should be doing.' The list of arrangements seemed dauntingly endless. 'And I'm sure you do too.'

'Not especially.'

She reached out and squeezed his hand. 'I really appreciate the thought, but I'm fine.' Theo's lean features clenched as he looked at the small hand covering his own.

'You are...' He stopped abruptly.

Puzzled by the odd intensity of his manner, Beth angled a questioning look up at his face.

He seemed about to say something but then the doorbell rang. The sound seemed to jolt him from some sort of reverie; he swore and pulled his hand from under hers.

'I'll get it.'

He returned a moment later with Muriel, the wife of the local vicar, a nice woman with a permanently harassed air but a kind heart.

Gran had been fond of her and Beth was genuinely pleased to see her.

'I heard. I am so sorry,' she said, enfolding Beth in a warm hug. 'I'll put on the kettle. Will your friend be staying?' she asked, looking curiously at Theo who, in his designer suit, did look very out of place in the kitchen, which had seen better days.

Out of place in her life.

Beth cut in quickly before Theo could respond. 'No, he was just leaving.'

Her eyes fell from his. Her life was too complicated right now; she did not want to make it even more problematical by seeing stuff that wasn't there.

Theo, she now realized, had been raised with a strong sense of duty and this was essentially a duty visit—no more, no less.

Theo left, promising to be back later. Beth took his comment to be one of those things people said when they were being polite; she definitely did not imagine he meant it literally.

It was with some surprise that she opened the door later that day to find him standing on the doorstep.

'I thought you might be hungry.'

Beth, who hadn't eaten all day, said, 'Not really.'

Theo gave her one of his sardonic looks and walked past her into the house.

'Come in, why don't you?' Beth shouted after him.

Actually, the place did seem less big and empty with him in it.

'You cooked this?' Beth stared in amazement at the cartons of food he was laying out on the table.

'I would like to take the credit but no, not me—Louis. He does not normally make home deliveries but I think he likes you. So sit, eat.'

'What about you?'

'I have eaten,' he said, dragging out a chair.

Beth directed a doubtful stare at him. 'Just what are you doing here, Theo?'

'Bringing food?' he suggested, gesturing to the table.

Beth still looked unconvinced.

'On this occasion I have no underlying sinister motive, though, naturally, if I did have I would not tell you.'

'Well, it is very…nice of you.'

The food was delicious and, as she ate, Beth realised that she had been ravenous. She paused, fork midway to her mouth, and looked at Theo. 'Are you going to watch every mouthful I eat because I have to tell you it's bad for my digestion.' And this food was nothing like the occasional Friday night Chinese she brought home.

He picked up a fork. 'In that case I might join you,' he said, diving in.

They ate in companionable silence, broken only when he revealed casually that Muriel would be staying the night.

Beth gave him a narrow-eyed stare but couldn't work herself up to real anger. She was actually relieved not to be spending the night alone in the big empty house with so many reminders. 'Whose idea was that?'

His eyes widened in unconvincing innocence. 'She insisted.'

'How did you come to be speaking to her in the first place?'

'I gave her my number. I often give attractive women my number. Sometimes they even call me.'

Beth fought a smile. 'Has anyone ever told you that you are a control freak?'

'Up until this moment, no.'

'Now,' he said when they had finished, 'you go and rest; you look ready to fall down.'

CHAPTER TWELVE

BETH argued but he ignored her protests that she wasn't tired. Eventually she humoured him and went to her bedroom, conscious, as she climbed the creaky stairs, of the doorbell ringing. She had reached the first landing when she heard voices, one deep, one loud.

Presumably it was her *babysitter*—crazy idea, but when he got something into his head the man was about as flexible as a steel bar. Aggravating, but she had to admit that steel bar characteristics did have their uses, especially during moments of crisis. And, if you had to choose a person to be around when your world fell apart at the seams, she could see why Theo might be many people's first choice.

It went against the grain to humour him but he had been kind of fantastic and she didn't have the strength to fight his ludicrous conviction she could not be left alone, but once he was gone she had every intention of re-establishing her independence.

As she lay on her bed Beth had no expectation of sleeping. The next thing she knew, it was five hours later. She checked the bedside clock with her watch, unable to believe it was that late. She remembered lying down and then nothing—a blissful mind-numbing blank.

She swung her legs over the side of the bed and sat up groggily. The cold water she splashed on her face made her feel slightly more human; it washed away the drowsiness but also the last remnants of her make-up, revealing the dark, bruised-looking shadows under her eyes and scary pallor of her skin.

With a grimace of distaste, she looked down at her creased and crumpled clothes; she had slid under the quilt fully clothed earlier and it showed.

Fighting the lethargy that made everything seem an effort, she undressed and stepped into the shower. Unable to work up any enthusiasm to select fresh clothes, she pulled on an old towelling robe over her bra and pants and slid her feet into a pair of fluffy slippers.

Beth's nostrils twitched. The smell of fresh coffee permeating the draughty old house suggested that the vicar's wife had indeed arrived.

Despite her earlier misgivings about being in the house on her own, partly due, she suspected, to sleep deprivation, all she actually wanted was to be left alone. On the way downstairs she rehearsed the speech in her head, the one that was going to convince Muriel Baxter that, no matter what Theo had told her, she really didn't need a babysitter.

She walked into the kitchen wearing an expression that she hoped would demonstrate that she was not about to fall apart.

The expression peeled away when she found not the vicar's middle-aged wife but Theo, sitting at the scrubbed kitchen table with work spread out in front of him.

'What are you still doing here?'

Then, conscious that her accusing tone was not really appropriate when she was talking to someone who had been far more generous with his time than common courtesy demanded, she added awkwardly, 'I thought you'd be at work.'

'I had meetings—they were cancelled.' He saw no need to explain that he had done the cancelling because she might misread the gesture.

And it had not been any major inconvenience. His actions had not been compelled by pity or compassion; they had been of a purely practical nature. He could not give his full attention to the items under discussion when he was distracted by the thought of Beth waking in this big empty house alone.

Obviously, he was not responsible for her but to walk away right now would be, to his way of thinking, just as unacceptable as walking away from the scene of an accident.

'Muriel…?'

Theo watched as she looked around the big room— Victoria had still been on the throne when it had its last refurb—as though the vicar's wife might be hiding in a dresser cupboard.

'She had an emergency at home.' The woman had been apologetic after she'd received the phone message and her explanation garbled. Frowning, he recalled the gist of their conversation. 'I believe one of her children fell off, or possibly into something.'

'That would be George,' Beth said, tightening the belt on her robe. 'He is sort of a legend, an accident-prone ten-year-old,' she added when he looked blank. 'I hope he's all right,' she added worriedly.

Theo closed the laptop that lay open on the big scrubbed table and slid his phone back into his pocket. 'I did not get the impression it was anything life-threatening or even serious and, should you require it, Muriel asked me to tell you that her sister-in-law will come and sleep the night here if you wish.'

It was churlish, she knew, to feel irritated when everyone

had the best possible intentions but she was getting tired of being treated as though she was helpless. 'That's very kind, but I'd actually prefer to be alone and I'm sure everyone—' her glance flickered significantly to his belongings on the table '—has things to get on with.'

'People are concerned.'

Beth's jaw tightened. Couldn't he see this was his opportunity to leave, any obligation he might have felt fully discharged?

Circumstances had conspired to throw them together and she doubted he was any happier about it than she was, which made his continued presence even more inexplicable.

What was holding him here?

Not a desire for her company, Beth was sure. He'd toned down the antagonism, presumably in deference to her bereavement, but, if anything, the uneasiness she had always felt in his presence had actually intensified.

'And I'm grateful.' Her lashes swept downwards. She would have preferred to owe the debt of gratitude to anyone but him. 'But, as you can see, I'm fine.'

Beth regretted inviting his searching scrutiny, but she withstood it as best she could, even though her reaction to his dark clinical stare had a less than clinical effect on her stomach muscles.

She did not look fine. Composed, yes, but fine, no, he decided, studying the fine lines of strain around her soft mouth and the pain in her eyes.

Despite the fact she was clearly capable, he still felt a strong reluctance to leave her in this place with so many memories. 'This house is…'

Reading the criticism in his encompassing gesture and frown, Beth lifted her chin to a defensive angle and jumped in angrily before he could complete his sentence.

'My home—and I have been living here alone for some time.'

The mental image of her, arriving home to this vast, empty, half-derelict shell, made Theo feel inexplicably angry. 'Insanity.'

Beth looked at him and saw all the people who'd been offering her very sound financial advice, people who understood figures but who didn't have a heart.

Hands clenched at her sides, her contemptuous gaze came to rest on his face, even in her anger registering the aesthetic harmony in his sternly delineated features—the slashing cheekbones, the aquiline moulding of his nose, his dark bold stare and the innate sensuality of his lips.

'I suppose you'd sell this place to a developer who would divide it up into *sympathetic* conversions and sell off the garden for them to cram in—what would you say—twenty units and garages in the vegetable plot?' Her shaking voice rose to an angry shrill shout.

'Is that an option?' It sounded to him like a good one. Even in this market, the house values in this upmarket and very desirable location were still on the rise.

'Over my dead body!'

His brows lifted at her vehemence. 'Living in damp conditions like this, it is not an impossible outcome.'

Her eyes narrowed. 'Don't be so dramatic!' she snapped, making a point of ignoring the chair he pulled out and stalking instead to the other side of the room.

The accusation, from someone who had just thrown her rattle out of the pram and indulged in a hissy fit for no reason he could fathom, struck him as amusing. It was incredible, Theo mused as he watched her, how eloquent a back could be; he found the anger and antagonism Beth's stiff shoulders and slender rigid back screamed infinitely preferable to the weary defeat her body language had projected earlier in the day.

If yelling at him made her feel better, Theo had no objections. His skin was pretty thick.

He nudged the rotting skirting board with the toe of his shoe. 'You know you have dry rot here.' And, though it was the only place he'd seen physical evidence, Theo was pretty sure that this sad, neglected building had every sort of rot known to man. Without this money pit, Beth could buy herself a small place and have money left in the bank as security. 'Financially, the most profitable course would be to demolish and—'

Beth swung back, fists clenched and eyes blazing. 'Now why am I not surprised to hear you say that?' She pressed a finger to her chin as she posed the question before loosing a scornful laugh and adding, 'Fortunately, we are listed.'

Apparently, at some point during this conversation he had become public enemy number one. He was fairly philosophical about the role that had been thrust upon him. 'Doesn't historical listing mean that you are legally obliged to maintain the fabric of the building?'

The comment he had considered innocuous had a red rag to a bull effect on Beth, who compressed her lips and regarded him with the warmth normally reserved for something that had crawled out from under a stone.

Theo was right, which obviously made her even more angry with him. Did he think she wanted to see the home she loved fall down from neglect? Did he have a clue how much the last quarter's electricity bill was?

She looked at him standing there, so smug, so secure and confident, not to mention gorgeous in his hand-made shoes. A hundred angry retorts flickered through her mind.

She opened her mouth to deliver one and stopped dead. *What am I doing?*

She was angry with Theo but the only thing he had been guilty of was kindness; she gave a shamed grimace.

Why was she still fighting for the house? When there was a chance Gran might come home there had been a reason for battling against the odds to keep it intact. Now there wasn't. Gran was never coming home, it didn't matter what happened to the place—it was just a building, bricks and mortar.

It was no longer, she realized, a question of *if* she sold but *when*.

'I hope you won't take this the wrong way, but what I want most now is to be left alone.'

His expression was dubious as he searched her face. As the silence stretched so did her conviction that he was about to refuse her request. So when he did agree without an argument, but on the strict proviso she use the number he left should she need anything, Beth felt a sense of anticlimax.

Her perverse response would only have made sense had she wanted him to stay.

Theo made it as far as the car before he realised he had left the keys in the house.

He lifted his hand to knock on the door but the defective latch had not caught and pushing it swung it inwards with a Halloween squeak. He grimaced at this fresh evidence of the house's decay; no insurance firm was going to pay up if there was a break-in with the state of this building's defences.

Theo felt his temper mount as he thought of Beth spending nights alone in a place that was an open invitation to any passing low life who would consider her easy prey.

He was not a man who allowed his imagination to run away with him but Theo was fighting a head full of nightmare images as he closed the door behind him; he would send a locksmith first thing in the morning.

The instant he walked into the kitchen, he knew his deliberate efforts to be noisy had been wasted. Beth's sobs would drown out a twenty gun salute, let alone his foot-stomping attempts to let her know he was there.

She was on her knees in the middle of the room, her face buried in a bundle of blue woollen fabric, sobbing her heart out.

Watching her, listening to her, Theo felt as though someone had reached into his chest and grabbed his heart. The heart-rending sounds made the skin on his scalp tingle; each successive sob tightened the grip of the icy fingers around his heart.

Either he made a sound or some sixth sense alerted her to his presence, but Beth turned her head, her hair wafting across her tear-stained red face as she lifted her head.

Under her dark lashes, her eyes connected with his. Theo watched them widen, not with pleasure but dismay.

Some perverse part of him wanted her to smile when she saw him.

She dragged a hand across her damp face and sniffed. Visibly struggling to regain her composure, she got to her feet.

Theo looked at the crumpled garment she still clutched.

She caught the direction of his gaze. 'Gran's favourite cardie.' She put the damp woollen bundle on the table. 'It smelt of her.'

The muffled explanation set in motion a tidal wave of empathy that totally submerged him as her gold-flecked green eyes, filled with an ineffable sadness, meshed with his.

* * *

'I left my car keys.' The desire to gather her in his arms and tell her everything was going to be all right, even if it wasn't, was almost overwhelming. A natural human instinct to offer comfort, he told himself, and one that he resisted.

A hug might start out as comfort but there was enough sexual charge in the air between them that meant it might end up as something else. Normally, he would not have been concerned but his normally reliable restraint had developed a few cracks.

Feeling more utterly foolish than she ever had in her life, Beth watched through her damp lashes as he retrieved his key ring from the table. She hated that it had been Theo who had witnessed her meltdown.

'Scents are very…evocative,' he agreed, thinking of the womanly floral scent of her body.

She looked up into his lean, darkly devastatingly handsome face and smiled before she blew out a gusty breath and said, 'Right, goodbye again and thanks.'

Standing there with the plucky smile painted on her face, she looked incredibly fragile. Theo could see her composure was paper-thin; the gutsy act she was putting on was for his benefit.

Was this display bravery or was it just sheer stubborn independence? Well, either way, it only increased the protectiveness that rose up in him when he looked at her… She was so damned fragile.

'I could call Andreas.'

The suggestion made her stiffen. Anger coursed through her and Beth embraced it. 'I actually thought you were being nice.' *First mistake, Beth. The second was starting to feel grateful.* 'Now, how stupid does that make me? Oh, in case you were wondering, that was a rhetorical question.'

She already knew the answer.

While she'd thought he was being kind, that he cared,

he was simply working out how to use this situation to his own advantage.

'I don't suppose someone like me is even a person to you!' she flung. '*My* mistake,' she added bitterly. 'I forgot what sort of person I'm dealing with; you're a self-centred manipulative pig. Well, for the record, if you want your brother's girlfriend you'll have to get her without my help because I'm not playing any more.' Breathing hard, she made a symbolic gesture of wiping her hands clean of them.

'It never occurred to me that you would be...*playing*. In my opinion, you should not be alone here. I mentioned Andreas because I thought you might find his company preferable to mine.'

His calm response deflated her bubble of righteous anger.

'Elizabeth, you shouldn't be alone.' Theo took a step towards her, hand outstretched.

Rejecting the sympathy she saw reflected in his dark eyes, Beth backed away, both hands lifted in a protective barrier as she growled, 'Just go away and leave me alone.' She stopped and gulped before adding huskily, 'Please, Theo, just...' She stopped, her eyes clinging to his dark lean face, breathing hard. Then, with a tiny groan, she flung herself across the space separating them.

Theo stood still, barely breathing, his body rigid as she reached up, grabbed his head between her hands and, raising herself on tiptoe, her slim body shaking as she plastered herself up against him to reach her goal and she pressed a hard kiss to his mouth.

She stepped away, feeling almost as shocked as he looked that that she had followed through with the wild, crazy impulse.

She just said one word. '*Go!*'

Without a word, Theo turned, his painful arousal making it hard for him to walk in a straight line. It had taken every ounce of his self-control and some more not to kiss her back, not to gather her in his arms and crush her soft body into his, hunger still roared like an out of control fire in his veins.

Beth watched him walk to the door, the voice in her head screaming—*don't go*. She opened her mouth to call out but nothing came out. He had opened the door when the words came.

'Don't go!'

CHAPTER THIRTEEN

THE husky cry made Theo freeze in his tracks. He turned slowly and began to walk back to where she stood, looking small and fragile but wearing an expression of reckless bright-eyed determination.

Her knuckles stood out, bloodless white, as she knitted her hands and begged, 'Stay with me.'

He gritted his teeth as he fought his primal response to the invitation; it roared in his blood as he kept his expression neutral and said, 'I'll get Muriel's sister-in-law.'

Beth frowned, tears of sheer frustration standing out in her eyes as she shook her head. 'That's not what I meant.'

Theo, who knew it was not what she meant, continued to pretend ignorance. Acknowledging what she was saying would make the impossible even harder. The temptation of responding to the beseeching plea in her eyes was so great that Theo had to take several deep breaths before he trusted himself to respond.

'I can't.'

Her lips trembled and tears spilled from her luminous eyes. 'You could but you don't want to!'

But he had wanted to, she thought, the muscles low in her pelvis tightening as she recalled the hard imprint of his erection pressing into the softness of her belly. She might not know much but she knew he had wanted her when she'd kissed him.

'That is not the point.' Theo could feel the cold sweat standing out in beads across his forehead as he fought to retain control. 'You are upset and you are vulnerable.'

His burning glance dropped to her provocatively pouting lips and he realised that he had never wanted to possess a woman more in his life—it was consuming him from the inside out.

'I am trying to do the right thing here,' he told her, clinging on to his principles with his fingernails. 'And tomorrow you will thank me for it,' he predicted hoarsely.

'Don't tell me how I feel,' Beth flared angrily. She raised her hand, never sure, in retrospect, if she actually intended to lash out in frustration.

Before she could follow through with anything, he caught her hand tight, his fingers curling around her wrist, pulling it against his heaving chest.

Beth froze. His lean body was racked by tremors; she could feel them rippling through his body in waves.

The leashed strength and controlled power she sensed in him excited her more than she would have imagined possible. Everything about him, from his sheer undiluted raw masculinity to the sinful curve of his marvellous mouth excited her.

She closed her eyes and breathed in the scent of him.

'*Elizabeth*.' He slurred her name in a heavily accented growl.

She opened her eyes and stared up at him, longing in her face as he slid a hand into her hair, letting the silky skein fall through his fingers.

Beth watched the muscles in his brown throat work as he swallowed hard. He lifted his head and ran a not quite steady hand back and forth over his hair.

'I'm going to call the vicar's wife and get her to ask her sister-in-law to stay the night, then—'

'You want me.' The certainty sent a wave of relief through her.

'Beth…'

The warning note in his voice had no effect on Beth's intentions. She tilted her head back to look him in the face, raised herself on tiptoe and linked her fingers behind his neck.

Theo tried to look anywhere but at her but he was drawn to her face as she fixed her clear gaze on him. 'You want me,' she said again very softly.

The dull thud in his head was like a metronome. 'Elizabeth, you—' She laid a hand against his lips and, with a groan that she felt vibrate through his body, Theo opened his mouth and kissed her palm.

The moist, warm contact sent a deep shiver through her body.

Again, he shook his head and tried to step back. Beth slid her fingers into his hair. 'Please, Theo, I just need not to think, not to feel…I want it all to go away for a little while. I know you could do that for me.' She looked up at him, the light from the lamp giving an alabaster sheen to her pale skin, unable to explain the instincts that drove her.

He nodded slowly and she felt a quiver run through his lean hard body, but still he held back. 'I know you want to block out the pain but it will still be there.'

'I know, but give me this one night.'

He sucked in a breath through flared nostrils and fought to take control of his rampaging hormones. Deep inside, he sensed that the fight was already lost but, conscious that her vulnerability put her out of reach, he held on, if not to his sanity, at least to his principles.

'Look, you're feeling a lot of things right now that—'

She lifted her chin and cut across him. 'Do not patronise me, Theo. I'm not a ch…child.' She bit her quivering lower lip. When she had asked him to stay she had genuinely not anticipated rejection. 'You don't want me—it is no problem.'

Theo held a groan behind clenched teeth as he watched her give a pathetically unconvincing shrug of unconcern.

'I just wish you'd say so instead of pretending to be noble.'

Something snapped inside Theo; there was a red mist before his eyes as, with a low growl vibrating in his throat, he lunged forward and reached for her. Grabbing her by both wrists, he turned her round and jerked her into his body.

The impact with his rock-hard body sent the breath from Beth's lungs. She tilted her head back and they stood there, both breathing hard as they stared into each other's eyes

'I am not noble!'

But he was, she decided, beautiful. 'Good,' she said, unable to hide her relief.

Theo raised her hands to his lips, kissing the blue-veined inner aspect of her narrow wrists before he freed them.

He stroked her face with the pad of his thumb before pushing his fingers into her hair. Beth stood, unable to move, simply able to feel sensation coursing through her body as he slowly lowered his mouth to hers.

She felt her shaking knees give as he kissed her hard, one hand cupping the back of her head, the other framing her face. She grabbed a handful of shirt to hold herself upright as she opened her mouth beneath his.

She moaned low in her throat as his tongue slid into her mouth. He began to lift his head and Beth panicked. 'Don't stop!'

The plea sent a ripple through his tense, primed body. *'I can't.'*

Seeing his face through a haze of dancing heat, the expression of driving urgency stamped on his dark features as his big hands closed around her narrow ribcage made Beth's control slip several more notches.

She thought *what control?* and gasped as he lifted her with no apparent effort off the ground so that their faces were level.

'Kiss me!' he commanded.

Beth did and felt him groan low in his throat and she met his tongue with her own. Her hands were wound tight around his neck as they both strained to deepen the pressure, kissing with frenzied feverish hunger.

The heat and hardness of his lean virile body seeped through the layers of clothes that separated them. Beth's starved senses soaked up the impressions like a vacuum sucking in air; it was utterly and totally intoxicating. There was no room for anything else in her mind—just Theo.

Her entire body hummed with excitement. Beth was breathless and shaking with the intensity of it; it pooled, thick and hot, between her thighs. Each fresh stabbing incursion of his tongue sent her deeper into the sensual maelstrom she was suspended in.

'Oh, God!' she whispered against his mouth. 'You taste so good.' She ran her fingers over the dark stubble on his jaw, enjoying every single sensation, hungry to discover all of him.

He replied, speaking in his native tongue, the words spilling from his lips with erotic throaty passion that sent electrical tingles shimmering along Beth's nerve endings.

'Look at me!'

It was a struggle to respond but Beth prised her heavy

eyelids open and the febrile glitter she saw glowing like hot embers in the darkness of his eyes made her senses spin.

'Say my name, I want to hear you say my name...'

Considering she was in the grip of a newly discovered need to please him and felt almost a compulsion to satisfy any demand he made, she felt strangely shy complying with his modest request.

She slid her hands over his shoulders, exploring and revelling in the rock-hard solidity and strength of the muscles there before framing his face between her hands. 'Theo,' she said.

The expression in her eyes when she said his name dragged like a weight at his heart.

'Theo, are you going to take me to bed?'

His pupils dilated dramatically as he turned his head, a feral moan leaving his lips as he pressed a kiss to her palm and shook his head. 'Too far,' he slurred, unable to articulate the depth of urgency in his blood. He kissed her again, bending her head back, exposing the long lovely line of her pale neck.

He was shaking with the need that consumed him as he lifted her into his arms, soft and warm and smelling like the very essence of femininity.

They continued to kiss as he carried her over to the old saggy sofa beside the old-fashioned blacked range, but Beth was oblivious to the broken spring digging into her back as he laid her down.

One foot braced on the floor, his big body curved over her. As she gazed up at this big beautiful man looking down at her, his smoky eyes dark with desire, Beth's senses leapt and things deep inside her shifted and tightened, the heat spreading out from the tight hot core low in her belly until she was burning.

She felt both overwhelmed and excited, wanting him

close, wanting to feel his skin, taste his skin—wanted with a raw urgency that scared and thrilled her.

His fingers shook as they slipped the tie on her robe. Peeling back the fabric to expose her body, he caught his breath.

'You are beautiful,' he rasped, cupping one small perfect breast in his hand, his thumb rubbing across the peak straining against the lacy covering before pushing it back to reveal the smooth perfection of first one small quivering mound and then the other.

Holding her eyes, he fought his way out of his shirt.

Beth watched as his ribcage rose and fell. Broad of shoulder, the muscles of his upper body were perfectly formed, his skin glowed a deep Mediterranean gold—he was utterly gorgeous. Beth gasped as he lowered himself onto her, flattening her sensitised breasts against his bare chest.

He kissed her as though he'd drain her, until she barely knew where he ended and she began.

The heat in her blood hummed as he groaned, 'I want to taste all of you.'

Beth closed her eyes tight as he kissed his way down her body, caressing her with his hands. She gasped as he pushed back the lacy covering to reveal all of her; when he took her into his mouth she thought she would die from the sheer pleasure of it.

Her control snapped totally as she reached for him. Her teeth clenched, her flushed face a mask of fierce need, she was almost sobbing with frustration as her fingers fumbled frantically at the buckle of his belt.

'It's all right,' he soothed.

'I need this…you…now…I want…I don't want to feel anything…just you…' She shook her head back and forth in frustration at her inability to express the instincts that drove her.

'I know,' he told her thickly, catching her face between his thumb and finger. 'I really do know.' He took her hand, fed her fingers onto the straining ridge along his zip and groaned as her fingers tightened over the pulsing outline of his erection.

The heat pulsing between her legs drew a feral moan from Beth but, before her exploring fingers could satisfy the carnal curiosity coursing in her veins or shred Theo's control any further, he levered himself slightly off her and finished the job she had begun.

The metallic sound of his zip introduced a tiny flicker of sanity into Beth's passion but it vanished the moment he joined her again, hard and solid, his weight pressing down onto her deliciously. The sheen of sweat that glistened on his golden skin and clung to the drift of dark body hair on his chest delineated every ridge of hard muscle.

She reached for him, her eyes widening, as he took her wrists and closed her fingers around the wooden backrest of the sofa. Being exposed to his hot gaze made her feel—*liberated*? Before she could even begin to ponder this development, she got totally sucked into the hot passion seething in the air; she was so aroused she could barely breathe.

His stillness had an explosive quality as he looked into her painfully expressive eyes before allowing his glance to slide slowly over the naked curves of her pale slender body.

As he gazed at her lying there, exposed and open for him, so soft and warm, so totally *her*, he thought—*you belong with me*, a primal truth for the complicated feelings seething inside him, and a truth without the benefit of logic, but Theo realised he believed it to his core and to recognise it was almost a relief.

He kissed her hard, nipping into the soft lushness of her

lips as he spread her legs and insinuated his hair-roughened muscular thighs between them.

Beth's hands tightened on the wooden arm rest for a second before she let go and grabbed for him. Her hands glided over the satiny skin stretched damply across the bunched muscles of his shoulders, searching for purchase. She turned her face into his neck, kissing his salty skin as she closed her eyes, feeling the unbelievable mind-numbing excitement of having him, thick and throbbing, between her thighs.

They were both breathing hard and fast as he whispered her name, his sweat-slick body shaking as he slid into her in one smooth thrust.

Beth's body arched under him, her eyes flying wide as she released a shocked cry. 'Oh, God, you're...' The searing sweetness of the sensation coursed through her body.

Above her, Theo froze, shock etched into every plane and angle of his taut features. She was tight and hot around him—very tight. 'It's fine,' he soothed.

'No, not fine.' The astonishing sensation of being filled by Theo was a million miles from *fine*—it was shattering and incredible. It was pleasure on a mind-numbing scale. 'This is...*you* are...oh, God, just so good, Theo.'

The awareness that he was her first lover primitively excited and horrified Theo in equal measure, though, as she squirmed beneath him, excitement took the upper hand.

'Slowly,' he urged, easing himself from the tight silken grip of her body.

Beth's instinctive cry of protest was almost immediately transformed into a fractured moan of startled pleasure as he slid back into her.

She lifted her hips instinctively to meet him as Theo repeated the process over and over until the heat was everywhere inside her—under her skin, the soles of her feet—her entire body was taken over by the process.

She buried her face in his neck, biting into the muscled column as he drove deeper and deeper until she felt she would dissolve; her body simply could not withstand this level of mind-shattering pleasure.

Tormented by the feeling that she was reaching for some ultimate pleasure just out of reach, Beth's gasps and cries grew hoarser as she sank deeper into her own body, swept away by the wild exhilaration roaring in her blood.

When the first contraction hit her Beth stopped breathing as every cell in her body silently imploded. She gasped, every sinew and muscle from her toes to her scalp contracting as the successive waves of pleasure swept her away.

Above her, she was distantly aware of Theo reaching the same plateau and exploding hotly within her.

Beth felt no desire for him to move as he lay on top of her, breathing hard. She enjoyed the intimacy, the weight of him, the musky scent of sex on his body.

The aftershocks still hit her intermittently, causing her to say his name and tighten her grip on his shoulders.

She could feel the waves of exhaustion that threatened to sweep over her but she was still very awake when he finally lifted his head and looked deep into her eyes.

She smiled and sighed, running a hand along the abrasive roughness of his jaw and whispered, 'Thank you.'

Theo watched her eyelids squeeze closed, saw the dampness seeping out from beneath the delicate folds and felt a wave of violent self-disgust.

He may not have known that she was a virgin—though, wise after the event, he could now see there had been strong indications—but he had known that she was vulnerable. That had not stopped him slaking his hunger at her expense.

She had needed hugging and holding, not sex.

The weight of his guilt lay heavily on his shoulders as Theo lifted her into his arms. She slept on, not stirring as he carried her curled trustingly in his arms—a trust that he did not deserve.

God, he hadn't even taken off his clothes; she had received none of the gentle consideration at his hands that a woman deserved the first time. No gentle seduction, candles, music—just thrown down on a dusty sofa and taken with a hungry impatience that made no concession to her inexperience.

By the time he had entered the first three rooms on the first floor—none showed any sign of habitation—in Theo's mind, his behaviour had become little better than that of a wild animal.

In the fourth, his luck turned. It held a single bed covered in a patchwork quilt, a bookcase and a chest of drawers; the rest of the clothes hung on a rail.

Another scan revealed that, though he was in a woman's room, there was no mirror, not even a reflective surface. Clearly, vanity was not one of Elizabeth's besetting sins and if she had ever gone through a rebellious period in her formative years there was no sign of it in this room; it was neat, tidy and, yes…virginal.

Forced to remove a battered stuffed toy that had seen better days before he could pull back the covers to lay her on the bed, Theo felt even more of a defiler of innocence.

She opened her eyes sleepily as he laid her down and continued to watch him though half closed eyes as he peeled off his clothes and joined her.

She curled up against him, her silky hair tickling his nose as she tucked her head under his chin and whispered, 'Thank you for staying,' before falling deeply asleep.

Theo could not recall the last time he had spent the entire

night with a woman; he was still awake when she woke around two a.m. Clearly emerging from a nightmare, she clutched at him, shaking, her body sweat-slick with fear that cooled as he stroked her.

The soothing became something else but this time Theo kept a tight rein on his passion. He made love to her slowly, the long slow burn testing his control but ensuring that, when it came, satisfaction was correspondingly intense.

Theo had never known pleasure like it and, in truth, he felt almost as marvellous as she told him he was.

The last time it was he who woke to Beth's hands on his body, her soft voice whispering huskily in his ear that this time he was hers.

This was not a plan he had a problem with.

CHAPTER FOURTEEN

WHEN Beth awoke the next morning Theo was already dressed. He sat, not a hair out of place, in the window seat, his suit somehow creaseless, his tie neatly knotted.

She looked at him and the control Theo had taken for granted his entire adult life slipped away, just like that. He had decided how to play it, had spent the early hours working out all possible scenarios in his head.

Now it was gone and he didn't have the faintest idea what he was going to say.

It was a minefield.

She had sex with him to block out the pain and because she was in a big empty house; she was hurting and she didn't want to be alone.

Not the most flattering reasons anyone had ever slept with him, but Elizabeth, he reflected with a tight smile, had a knack for deflating his ego.

His planned speech had run something along the lines of *when the pain goes away I will still be here and so will the sex and it will get better—the sex and the pain.*

It was not exactly a proposal but it was the nearest *thing* he had got to commitment in a long time and last night was the nearest he had got to magic—ever.

'You're awake.'

Beth watched him get to his feet and walk, tall and virile,

towards her. All the time she watched, inside her head a rerun of the previous night was playing.

He was a foot away when her face contorted in a grimace of sick self-disgust and she rolled over.

The guilt hit her.

It was like running full pelt into a brick wall.

Theo lost some colour as he watched her hit the pillow with her fist—presumably it was a stand in for his face. He had been anticipating some recrimination, but this...?

He opened his mouth and closed it again. How could he speak up in his defence when his behaviour had been, by definition, indefensible?

Beth stopped hitting the pillow and buried her head in it. She had nothing but utter contempt for her actions; she felt cheap. Her behaviour last night was a total betrayal of the lady who had taught her that if a person did not have self-respect she had nothing.

Gran, the one person in the world she cared for more than any other, had died and what had she done—cry, weep, spend some time remembering what a marvellous person she had been?

No, she'd shown her respect by ripping off Theo's clothes and begging him to have sex with her.

What sort of person did that?

She had never imagined that sex for the first time would involve virtually begging the man involved! No, there was no *virtually* involved—she had begged him.

Her first time and it had been sympathy sex.

And why Theo? She'd ruined her chance of having any sort of relationship with him, she realised. That thought was followed fast by the shocking realisation that she had wanted one.

The last couple of days she had learned several things, beside the fact that she was basically a cheap tart. Her supposed love for Andreas had been nothing more than a romantic crush; she had filled the blank in her life, not with a real man but a safer option—a man who was never going to return her feelings.

Then he had, or might have if she had wanted him to, and she had realised that the man she really wanted was his brother. A man even more unattainable, a man who had got under her skin from day one, a man who had always dominated her thoughts, even when he wasn't around.

A man she had ended up falling for.

Then she had begged him for sympathy sex.

Considering what she thought of herself this morning, she could only imagine what he was thinking of her!

'Will you just go away?' she yelled, her voice muffled by the pillow.

'Elizabeth?'

Beth gritted her teeth; she had to face him at some point. Dragging her hair back from her face with both hands, she rolled onto her back.

The direction of his gaze alerted her to her bare shoulders. Blushing, she dragged the sheet up to her chin.

'A little late for modesty, do you not think?'

Beth's eyes swept downwards, not seeing the smile that accompanied his words. She took a deep breath. 'Last night—'

'You were upset and—'

Beth cut him off with a wave of her hand; she was not interested in making excuses for herself. 'That doesn't matter. I'm just sorry it ever happened,' she sniffed.

The blood drained from his face.

Beth squeezed her eyes tight shut. 'I realise that respect is necessary in any sort of relationship.' She added with a laugh that sounded like a gulp, 'Not that we had a relationship as such.' And Theo would never respect her after last night, she thought sadly.

'We had sex.'

She flashed him a look. Did he think she'd forgotten? Beth half wished she had, but the experience would stay with her for ever, the impossibly perfect sex that she could never hope to recapture.

Actually, it was very possible she might never have any sort of sex ever again because the thought of anyone but Theo touching her that way made her feel ill.

'I really am ashamed and wish I could change it; I *really* wish *you* hadn't been here last night.'

The muscle beside Theo's mouth jerked as his jaw tightened. 'Who would you have liked to be here?' As if he needed to ask.

She looked at him in astonishment. The white-hot anger in his eyes made her recoil as he gritted through clenched teeth, 'Or is it a case of anyone but me? I may not be the man you wanted to be your first lover but I damn well am, and nothing will ever change that.' He threw the words at her like a challenge, turned on his heel and walked away.

It was a fortnight since the funeral and Beth had been back at work for ten days before she saw a member of the Kyriakis family—it was Daria.

She breezed into the office with a flustered Hannah, the girl who had transferred up from Accounts, following in her wake.

'Mrs Kyriakis, how nice to see you again.'

'My dear, please call me Daria.'

Beth was startled to find her eyes fill with emotional tears as she emerged from the warm hug.

'Let me look at you,' Daria commanded, taking a step back and surveying Beth from head to toe. From the verdict of, 'You poor, poor girl,' Beth assumed she looked terrible, though the compliments she had received recently on her new look suggested people less observant than Daria Carides noticed her clothes and hairstyle rather than the shadows under her eyes or the ten pounds she had dropped—her curves had virtually melted away.

It was just as well Daria had not seen her pre-makeover. She had been briefly tempted to adopt her old style but that would have been a step in the wrong direction—going backwards was not an option. Not that she had kept the clothes Theo had bought her. Instead, she had taken her old suits and blouses to a charity shop and bought several inexpensive but stylish alternatives from the High Street.

'You look exhausted. I'm so sorry I couldn't come to your grandmother's funeral. I hope Theo told you I was thinking of you—we all were.'

Beth's eyelashes swept downwards as she gave a non-committal smile. Theo had been there. She had seen him in the back of the church, then in the graveyard, a tall remote figure standing by himself, away from the main party of mourners, but he had not approached her.

Beth, in her turn, had ignored him totally. Maybe some people knew how to treat a man you'd begged to have casual sex with you but she was not one of them. She felt deeply ashamed that he'd occupied her thoughts on such an occasion but she was glad he had kept his distance, though the humiliating possibility that he might have done so because he was afraid she would expect a repeat of the sympathy sex did make her cringe.

'The flowers were lovely.' Beth lifted a slightly shaky hand to her hair; she had taken to wearing it loose but made a concession to the workplace by tucking it behind her ears. 'I'm afraid that Andreas is not here.'

'Oh, I know and, between ourselves, Ariana is not too

happy about this New Zealand trip of his. I had no idea it was on the cards, did you?'

Beth shook her head. She suspected that Andreas had had no idea either. The first she had known about it was when she had arrived at the office, only to be informed that Andreas was out of the country and she was in charge—just like that.

When she had protested that she wasn't qualified, the senior manager who had been holding the fort said the way he'd heard it she'd been virtually running the place anyway.

While this was an exaggeration, Beth did, after the initial blind panic, find she could cope. There had even been one or two moments when she had actually enjoyed herself and being busy was a welcome distraction. She'd begun to realise that it might even be difficult, once Andreas returned, to re-adapt to her old role as his assistant.

Though she was still no nearer knowing when that would be, if ever!

During the week, more details had emerged of the *big argument* that was spoken of in confidential whispers. Nobody knew what it was about, though there was much speculation, most of it—*big surprise*—surrounding Ariana, but it seemed that the brothers had had the granddaddy of all rows, after which Theo had stormed out of the building looking, according to one eyewitness to his departure, as sexy as sin.

'I just popped in to give you some details about the weekend.'

Beth looked at her blankly.

'The house party…?'

Beth, who had a vague recollection of something like that being mentioned during the awful dinner—which now seemed a lifetime ago—nodded cautiously.

'I've arranged for a car to pick you up directly from work on Friday.'

Beth's eyes widened in horror. The poor woman still thought she and Theo were an item. How was she going to break it to her that they never had been? It would probably be kinder to let her think they had just drifted apart. 'I'm afraid—'

Daria held up her gloved hand and shook her head. 'No, I simply won't take no from you as well. Both the boys have cried off and I've been looking forward to it for weeks. A little bit of sun and pampering is exactly what you need.'

If Daria was expecting sun, the woman really was an optimist; the radio that morning had forecast more of the same grey and gloomy weather they'd been enjoying for what seemed like forever.

'You do know that Theo and I aren't...'

'Theo won't be there,' his mother cut in.

Too busy taking of advantage of Andreas's absence and proving to Ariana he was the better brother? Beth reflected dourly.

'And my invitation is for you.' Daria broke off, her brow furrowed with concern. 'Are you all right, my dear? You look quite pale.'

'Fine,' Beth assured her as she breathed through the nausea and blinked away the images playing in her head. Theo could sleep with whoever he liked—it was nothing to her.

What was that saying—tell yourself something often enough and you'll end up believing it? Beth really hoped the person who coined that one had known what they were talking about.

The older woman gave a positive nod. 'You are *not* fine; I really must insist.'

The weak part of Beth wanted someone to insist,

someone to take the choices away, lift the responsibility that lay like a constant weight on her shoulders. She was tired of wills, bills, probate, death duty and people who wanted her declared unsound of mind because she wouldn't agree to have the garden of her childhood home sold off to developers, but she had been forced to agree to the sale of the house on the proviso that it was sold to people who would make it a family home.

It was no surprise that work had become her escape.

'I don't know if...' Beth grimaced, unable to disguise the fact that she was seriously tempted. 'This weekend?' The timing was kind of perfect. The estate agents had arranged a viewing for someone they saw as a serious potential buyer for the house that weekend and she'd been dreading it. If Theo wasn't going to be there...?

'I will have you back at your desk by Monday,' Daria promised with a beaming *done deal* smile.

'Thank you—that would be lovely.'

Daria got to her feet, enfolded Beth in another fragrant hug and said, 'I won't disturb you any longer.' She turned back at the door and said, 'I almost forgot. You don't have a problem with flying, do you?'

Beth looked at her blankly. 'No, but—'

'Excellent; it is possible to take a boat out but the helicopter is so much faster.'

Beth, struggling to follow, shook her head. 'Out to where?'

'Santos, of course.'

Beth's eyes flew wide. 'But I thought you lived in Kent.'

Daria smiled. 'Well, I do when we're in this country; we have a lovely little cottage there.'

Beth, her smile strained, nodded. She was getting the

impression that the Kyriakis version of *cottage* might equate with most people's idea of *mansion* or *castle*.

'We always hold my little family weekends on Santos and since his father died Theo has been more than happy for me to continue the tradition.'

Beth's smile stayed pasted in place until her visitor had departed.

Then, her expression dazed, she sat down with an audible thud that sent her chair spinning into the wall behind. She might have taken over Andreas's responsibilities but she had drawn the line at taking over his office.

She would be spending the weekend on a Greek billionaire's private island—now, how weird was that?

By most people's weirdness scale, she suspected it came below sleeping with said billionaire but Beth was not thinking of that.

And, once her cycle got back into sync after all the emotional trauma, she would be thinking about it even less. She had no idea why she was worrying. Things like that did not happen—not to her.

Ignoring the voice that said *denial* repeatedly in her head, Beth smiled. How Gran would have laughed, and she would also have encouraged her granddaughter to enjoy every moment of the experience.

Beth lifted her chin. She intended to do just that.

CHAPTER FIFTEEN

Two firsts in one day—a ride in a private jet and a helicopter trip across the Aegean. The latter left Beth's knees feeling a little shaky as she stood holding down her hair as the helicopter updraught tried to tug it out by the roots.

Beth looked around and thought *what next?*

Then she saw the figure striding towards her and the smile of anticipation faded from her face.

This is not happening, but it was and she had about thirty seconds to prepare herself for it.

Short of jumping off the nearby cliff and into the sea, she had no choice but to wait for him to reach her. She stood there, her eyes welded to his tall athletic figure, her heart throwing itself against her ribcage as if it was struggling to escape.

Play it cool, Beth.

The advice almost made her laugh; wild exhilaration and fear in equal quantities made playing it even tepid a non-starter. A fractured sigh slipped from her parted lips; the nervous tension that consumed her like a fever made her shake literally from head to toe as he approached.

Theo was going to take one look at her and know that she was aching with lust for him—he was going to look at her and she was going to tell him everything and she just wasn't ready!

'Elizabeth?'

He tipped his dark head in her direction and Beth just stared; it was almost a relief to stop fighting and accept that the only constant thing in her life was her feelings for him.

She loved him and that would never change.

'Theo, I've miss—' She stopped as a tall blonde figure stepped between them.

She had been so busy staring at Theo that she hadn't, until this moment, been aware of the woman with him. Her expression froze. Ariana's presence here—minus Andreas—did not necessarily mean she had switched brothers but it was a distinct possibility.

Beth closed her eyes and inhaled.

'You had a good journey?' Under the sweep of his ludicrously long lashes, Theo's dark, deep set eyes held no expression as they swept over her. 'You are ill?'

Beth took a deep breath and opened her eyes. 'Nausea, but it's passed. My first helicopter ride.'

She had seen him in formal clothes and no clothes but never before dressed casually. Wearing a white T-shirt and faded jeans, a shadow of stubble on his jaw and his short dark hair ruffled by the wind, he looked tanned and fit and perfectly at home, but then he *was* at home and she was the intruder.

'I didn't know you'd be h…here,' she said earnestly. 'Or I wouldn't have come,' she added quietly before turning her attention politely to the Greek woman.

'Hello, Ariana,' she said, forcing a smile.

The older woman was wearing an off-the-shoulder cropped T-shirt, very short shorts that showed lots of slim, tanned leg and very high spindly-heeled strappy sandals, none of which looked suitable for a trek along the rocky cliff path.

Ariana did not respond to her greeting, turning instead to Theo and voicing a loud complaint. 'I was stung! By a wasp—see.' She lifted up her T-shirt even higher to show Theo more of her smooth midriff.

'I can't see anything.' Theo barely glanced at her before he turned back to Beth.

She wouldn't have come if she'd known he was here.

They were not the words he had imagined hearing when he had played the scene in his head, but then neither had there been a third person in the scene.

He nodded towards her holdall and said, 'Is that all your luggage?'

'Yes, but I can carry it,' Beth said, snatching up the case before he could lift it.

'I'll carry it.'

Beth shook her head and insisted, 'It's not heavy.' Why was she making a big deal of this?

'It's half a mile to the house.' He put his hand over hers on the handle.

Beth pulled her hand away, gasping as an electrical pulse zapped along her nerve endings.

She saw him staring at her and said, 'Ouch—I snubbed my toe,' to cover the slip. Her determinedly cheerful smile grew even brighter as she added, 'A nice brisk walk will do me good.'

Theo levelled a critical gaze at her. 'You look like a nice brisk walk would kill you.' The short period since he had last seen her had taken its toll. Always fragile, she looked positively breakable.

Beth's lips tightened. 'Thanks very much; you sure knew how to make a girl feel good.' Then, remembering how good he was at making this particular girl feel a lot better than good, she felt a tide of warm colour wash over her skin.

He continued his censorious survey. 'What have you been doing to yourself?'

'You introduced me to fashion,' she reminded him, thinking *and a lot of other things*.

She struck a pose, sticking out her hip to display her jeans and brightly coloured T-shirt.

Theo's expression did not soften in response to the jokey action. 'I'm not talking about your clothes.' Her soft curves had vanished and in their place was an angularity that he found disturbing. 'You look like a puff of wind would blow you away.' Was she pining for Andreas? 'Have you been in contact with Andreas?'

It was Theo's cold, accusing manner as much as the seemingly unrelated question that made Beth blink in confusion. 'I sent him a couple of emails. There was a query about one of the accounts but things in the office are actually fine,' she added, wondering if he thought her presence here meant she was neglecting her new responsibilities.

'I do not wish to discuss the office.'

She looked up at him warily. 'You don't? You don't think someone more senior should be in charge?'

His eyes narrowed. 'Has someone been interfering? Because I gave instructions that you were to be given support but a free hand.'

Beth's eyes flew saucer wide. '*You* suggested me for the job?'

His autocratic smile flashed. 'I would not use the word *suggested*.'

'I'll try not to let you down.'

'Your work ethic or ability has never been in question, Elizabeth.' Her taste in men was. 'Andreas—he has not discussed his decision with you?' While Theo had been relieved that his brother had realised his engagement had been a mistake, this relief was tempered by the realisation that this decision left Andreas free to pursue Beth.

'What decision? And why would he discuss anything with me?' She frowned, alarm flashing into her eyes. 'If something has happened to Andreas I'd prefer you just told me.'

A muscle clenched in Theo's lean cheek as he flicked a look in Ariana's direction. 'Andreas is fine.'

Beth let out a gusty sigh of relief.

'He has somehow managed to muddle along without you.' And if he had any say in the matter he would continue to do so.

'I'm allergic!' Ariana, tired of being ignored, suddenly shouted, making them both turn. She pressed a hand to her chest. 'I think I'm having an anaphylactic shock.' She sank gracefully to the ground and moaned, 'Call an ambulance.'

With a sigh, Theo put Beth's holdall down and Beth promptly picked it up.

'Is it this way?' Without waiting for a reply, she set off along the path he had used. She had no desire to see Theo fussing around Ariana. The thought that he might be doing more than fuss sent a stab of jealousy through her aching heart.

After a few hundred yards the path forked. Beth barely paused before she took the right hand path; even if she got lost she didn't see how it could make the situation much worse than it already was.

Her fears that she might have missed the place proved misplaced—the Kyriakis house appeared around the next bend. It was a vast sprawling affair set almost into the cliff above the sea.

She was making her way towards the pillared main entrance when Theo caught her up.

'Where's Ariana?'

'Recovered,' he said shortly.

In a way, her unwelcome presence was his own doing. He now wished he had not insisted that Andreas break off his engagement in person and not, as his brother had intended, by email. Until he arrived, it would seem that they were stuck with Ariana.

'It was very kind of your mother to invite me.'

He stepped to one side to let her enter the house before him. 'My mother is a very kind woman.'

Beth looked around the space she found herself in. An entrance hall, but not as she knew it, it was vast and simply furnished, white walls and dark wooden floor scattered with rugs. The effect was one of space and coolness.

'She sends her apologies.'

Beth shook her head, not understanding.

'My mother sends her apologies. Georgios had an emergency at work. She managed to contact most of the other guests, except Ariana,' he added drily.

'And me.'

He tipped his head in acknowledgement.

This got worse. 'So there is no party.' Just a party for two and she was the gatecrasher. Feeling physically sick, she pressed a hand to her trembling lips. 'That's terrible. When can I arrange to go home?'

From her expression, it seemed to Theo that she looked capable of swimming if necessary. 'There is no transport back to the mainland until tomorrow and it need not be *terrible*.'

'Sure, because you really want *me* here.' She buried her face and groaned. 'Never mind. You can lock your door tonight as a safety measure. You and Ariana need not know I'm here; I can eat in my room and—'

His deep voice cut across her increasingly frenzied reassurances. 'What do I need protecting from?'

At that moment a man appeared. Theo spoke to him and, after nodding politely to Beth, he took her holdall away.

Theo turned back to Beth. 'So what do I need to lock my door against?'

'Me.'

'You?'

'In case I come begging for sympathy sex.'

An expression of utter astonishment crossed Theo's face, followed by comprehension. 'You think I fear you will beg me to make love to you?' His heated glance slid down her body. *Fear* would definitely not be his response if what she spoke of occurred.

Her chin fell to her chest. 'I won't,' she promised him in an earnest mortified whisper.

'You have no idea how relieved that makes me feel.'

This was Theo at his most sardonic and, puzzled by the ironic inflection in his deep voice, her head came up.

His thoughts flickered back over that fateful conversation. 'This is the shame you spoke of that morning?' At the time, her comment had cut him bone-deep and each time he had recalled the words since the pain had not lessened.

She nodded, her eyes sliding from his. 'You must think me a totally awful person,' she began huskily.

He arched a brow and felt a swell of tenderness as he looked into the face turned up to his. 'Why must I think this, *agape mou*?'

Beth's eyes widened. Was he joking? 'Gran was not even buried and I was—'

Theo's chest swelled as a wave of utter relief washed over him. His hand fell to her shoulder. 'I think that you would find that most people would not find your actions despicable, but mine. You asked, yes, but I did not need to say yes. I took advantage of you.'

It was Beth's turn to be astonished. 'But you didn't do anything I didn't want you to.'

Their eyes met and clung. Without thinking, she turned her face into his hand and closed her eyes as she felt his thumb move across the curve of her cheek. All she could hear was the banging of her heart as it threw itself against her ribs.

'And do you still?'

Beth swallowed past the emotional occlusion in her throat and opened her eyes. 'Yes, Theo,' she whispered.

A smile of primal male satisfaction split his lean features.

'The heel has come off my shoe.'

Beth jumped guiltily and wondered how long the woman had been standing there and how much of their conversation she had heard.

Beside her, she heard Theo swear. 'This situation is...' He stopped, making a visible effort to control his feelings. 'I told you they were unsuitable but you insisted on coming.'

'For a walk, not a run.'

Theo clenched his teeth and fought to control the swell of frustrated anger that made him want to forget the code of hospitality that compelled him to be at least basically civil to this unwanted guest.

'Perhaps you should take a rest. If you would excuse me, I have some calls to make.'

Just one, to his brother. He was going to suggest that Andreas brought forward his proposed flight from New Zealand—no, he was going to *insist* that he did.

Jaw taut with determination, he tipped his dark head to

the two women and saw the look of disappointment that Beth struggled to hide.

He took her chin in his hand, tipping her heart-shaped face up to him. 'Do not,' he said, fixing her with a look that made her heart leap, 'move from that spot. I will be back directly.'

Beth, oblivious to the flash of anger on the older woman's face as she silently observed the interchange, nodded her agreement to this fierce command and watched him stride away with a stunned expression. Things were happening so fast that she was finding it difficult to keep up.

'Long journey?'

Beth shook her head to clear her thoughts and responded to the older woman's bright enquiry with a vague nod.

'I know the perfect remedy for jet lag.'

'I'm not actually jet-lagged.'

Ariana acted as though she had not spoken. 'A nice swim. There's a lovely little cove just at the bottom of the cliff path.'

The woman appeared to be making a genuine effort to be friendly and, actually, a swim did sound rather nice. Beth smiled and admitted, 'That does sound tempting, but Theo has…' She paused, her eyes dropping as she added awkwardly, 'Plans.' What his plans might include sent a secret shiver of anticipation down her spine.

The older woman looked amused. 'He didn't mean wait literally; you do know that?'

Beth blushed and lied. 'Of course.' Presumably there was such a thing as looking too eager and possibly standing in the same place waiting for an hour or more fell into that category.

'Where is this beach? Do I follow the path…?'

'Don't worry, I'll show you the way. Here, in two minutes? Oh, I think Anton is waiting to show you your room.'

She spoke briefly to the man standing at the bottom of the flight of curving stairs. 'Yes, he'll take you up. Lucky you—you've got the VIP suite. Wait,' she added with a tight smile, 'until you see the view.'

It turned out she was right about the view—it was absolutely breathtaking—but, conscious of her promise to meet the Greek woman, she did not spend long enjoying it.

Pulling on a towelling robe over her swimsuit, she went down to find Ariana waiting for her.

'Won't Theo wonder where we are?'

'Oh, he knows everything that goes on here. He's a sort of king of the island—everyone reports to him.'

The other woman was so friendly that Beth began to wonder if she had previously done her an injustice. The beach in question was every bit as pretty as Ariana had suggested.

Beth, who stared longingly at the turquoise expanse, was surprised when the Greek woman, who had already peeled off a floor-length silky kaftan to reveal a minuscule bikini and a taut, well cared for body, laid out a towel and arranged herself on it.

'You're not swimming?'

'No, you go ahead. I need to top up my tan.'

Leaving her companion, Beth walked out into the water; it was delicious and beautifully warm against her skin. She waded in waist-deep, waving back to the shore and the watching woman before she struck out.

Beth classified herself as a competent rather than strong swimmer but, she reasoned, as long as she swam parallel to the shore there would be no problem.

When they had told him both women had gone to the beach Theo was surprised, not alarmed. Then they had reluctantly told him which beach—the one beach on the island that he still avoided.

Theo was walking down the cliff path when he saw her.

He hit the ground running. It was a desperate feeling to be able to see exactly what was happening but to be too far away to prevent it.

He broke all records reaching the beach.

When Ariana saw him the panic on her face might, in other circumstances, have been funny.

Theo, who was kicking off his shoes, did not waste time on words; his comments were brief but effective.

'Too far this time,' he said. He added grimly, 'Do not be here when I get back,' as he kicked his jeans away. 'And if anything happens to her there will be no place you can hide.'

He did not bother looking back to see if she had followed his advice. He waded to mid-thigh before diving into the surf.

He could not see her but he knew that by now Beth would have felt the drag of the current; she was probably trying to swim against it.

Even a very good swimmer who did not know that the only way out of the current was to swim with it rather than fight it, then at the right moment duck under it, would have exhausted their reserves of energy trying to escape within minutes.

He was a good swimmer and he did possess the vital local knowledge. So, as he swam out to her, Theo did not allow himself negative thoughts. She would be safe, he would not allow any harm to come to her and he would not return to shore without her.

When she saw him, Beth was utterly spent.

She opened her mouth to call his name and went under.

She came back up a moment later, spluttering and choking and he was there. In her panic she clutched at him, sending them both under this time.

'Relax, I've got you and let go of my neck—I need to breathe.'

Beth's panic receded but did not go away.

'I'm going to drown,' she said, releasing her stranglehold.

Theo ignored her doom-laden prediction, wrapped a strong arm around her ribs and flipped onto his back, pulling her on top of him. 'This is my watch—no one is going to drown today. Do you trust me, Elizabeth?'

Beth felt herself relax—it was a no-brainer. 'Yes.'

She followed his instructions, which amounted pretty much to do nothing besides not panicking, and a short time later he was dragging her out of the water.

Theo rolled onto his back, turned his head and looked at her as he said between pants, 'You all right?'

She nodded and crawled a few more feet before she flopped, face down, onto the sand. She lay there for several minutes, eyes closed, dragging air into her lungs in shuddering shallow gasps before she could summon the energy to even whisper, 'Thank you.'

'You are welcome.' Theo hauled himself into a sitting position. Now she was safe, he allowed himself to think about how close a call it had been. Though thinking was not really an adequate description of his *visceral* response to the knowledge that he had nearly lost her before he had ever had the chance to say *I love you*.

'Are you going to yell at me? Because I have to warn you that if you do I might well cry and it is not a pretty sight, as you probably remember.'

'I remember everything,' he rasped. 'I remember how you felt in my arms, how soft your skin was, how sweet you tasted, how tight you were around me. I remember everything and I have not thought of anything else since that night.'

She felt his passionate words in her bones, hotter than the sun that beat down on them. Unable to shake the feeling that this was all happening to someone else, she opened her eyes and saw his dark face close to her own, close enough for her to see the individual lines that radiated from the corners of his eyes.

She lifted her hand to his cheek and whispered, 'I remember too.'

'You're a beautiful sight.'

Not an accurate statement, but Beth did not feel inclined to protest. She didn't protest when he put his hand behind her head and dragged her mouth to his either.

The kiss lasted a long time and when it stopped they didn't move, just lay there staring at one another and breathing hard.

'You saved my life,' she whispered.

'I love you. I would have saved your life anyway, not being the total scum you appear to think I am, but loving you made it a priority.'

Beth just stared at him, wondering if the near death experience had made her hallucinate. Things were turning distinctly surreal.

'I don't think you're scum.' She thought *you're incredible* and felt her eyes fill with tears.

'Good. I have problems expressing my feelings.'

He'd had to tell her because she'd nearly died without knowing and that would have been... Theo thought *she nearly died* and felt that icy-cold fist clutch in his belly.

The memory he refused to acknowledge surfaced and he sucked in a breath and thought *Niki died and I couldn't save him.*

She blinked and said, 'You're a man; men don't express.'

Theo turned his head. Her hair, coated in sand, lay in a wet tangled halo around her face. His breath caught; she looked so beautiful.

'But, by way of compensation, I'm an excellent kisser.' He proceeded to demonstrate just how good.

Some time later Beth lay on her back in the sand watching Theo through the mesh of her lashes as he retrieved his phone from the pile of his clothes and issued some instructions.

He walked across to her looking so incredible that the breath caught in her throat. He held out his hand. 'There will be a doctor waiting at the house to check you over.'

Beth allowed him to haul her to her feet.

'The thing you said about loving me...' She angled a wary look up at his face. 'You did say that?'

'I did.'

The tender smile playing about his lips made her heart thud. 'And you meant it?'

'Every word.'

'I love you too.'

An expression of triumph blazed across his face as the tension left his shoulders. 'Well, thank God for that.'

He sealed his mouth to her own and Beth felt the weeks of hopeless longing, the nights of pent-up hunger and frustration slip away.

When he finally stopped kissing her, Theo stroked her cheek with a tenderness that brought tears to her eyes, his lips just a whisper away from hers, his warm breath warm on her cheek.

It was the water that lapped around their feet that made him finally release her. Laughing, Beth ran a little way up the beach. She turned back, expecting to see him behind her, but he hadn't moved. He stood there, staring out to sea with an expression on his face that drew her back to his side.

She laid a tentative hand on his shoulder. He turned his head and smiled, but the shadow in his eyes remained.

'What is it?' she asked, brushing away the dried sand that clung to his warm skin.

Theo shook his head and raised her hand to his lips.

'I know there's something.'

The breath left his lungs in a long sibilant rush as he turned his head and gazed back out to sea. 'I nearly lost you today before you were even mine.'

Beth looped her arms around his waist and pressed her slim body tight against the lean hard length of his. She brushed away the damp fabric of his shirt and kissed his chest.

'But you didn't lose me—I'm here.'

'No, I didn't, not this time.'

The enigmatic response made her brow pucker. He pulled away slightly and she angled a quizzical look at his face. 'This time?'

He took her hand and nodded. 'Come, let's walk and talk. I'll be happier when the doctor has looked at you,' he admitted. 'You can walk?'

'I'm fine.'

They had reached the path before he began to talk but, when he did, the words spilled from him in a flood. Beth had the impression they were things he had needed to say for a long time.

'You know I had an elder brother, Niki?'

Beth nodded, realising where this was going—his brother must have drowned and this had brought it all back.

His next words confirmed her suspicions, but it was worse—much worse.

'Everyone knows about the tides on the beach.'

Beth thought about Ariana, lying there watching her swim out, and shuddered.

'But we were kids and I never could resist a dare. Niki dared me. He didn't think I'd do it, but I did—I swam out. He swam out to get me but he got caught by the undercurrent too. I watched him go under and I couldn't do a thing about it.'

Beth's fingers tightened around his. The thought of him carrying this burden around with him made her heart ache—for the man he was and the boy he had been.

'Niki tried to save me, but somehow I got out and he drowned. I killed him.'

Beth stopped dead and pulled him back to face her. 'Of course you didn't—it was an accident.'

'That's what they said, of course, but I knew different.' And he knew that every time he looked at him their father had thought that the wrong son got taken by the sea.

He had never said it but Theo knew he had thought it.

'If I hadn't gone in...'

'If he hadn't dared you? What ifs are silly. Things happen—bad things happen—but you cannot carry this guilt around with you. Theo, you were a child. It was an accident. You have to let it go, in time.' A wound like his did not heal overnight, not when it had festered away for so long.

Theo gazed down into her earnest, lovely little face and felt his heart twist in his chest.

Beth gave a tentative smile and wondered what he was thinking.

'It is something I live with.'

Beth took the hand he held out and walked by his side, determined that while she was around she would try and lighten the burden he carried.

It was a long-term project and she didn't know how long she would be around.

So far, Theo had only admitted his feelings. There had been no mention of their enduring nature and he was not a man who did long-term relationships.

Beth pushed away the unanswered questions. The fact was, a week or a year, she intended to stay with Theo for as long as he wanted her because the alternative was unthinkable and, being an optimist, she could not dismiss the possibility that he might find she was enough variety for him.

CHAPTER SIXTEEN

THE doctor pronounced her fit and, after a private conversation with her on another subject, he was able to offer her some reassurance and the promise that he would bring the necessary test kit with him the next day.

She emerged after the examination to find Theo pacing up and down a balcony with stunning sea views. Also, she realised as she joined him, an excellent view of the helipad.

'Is someone arriving?' she asked, raising her voice above the mechanical noise carried in their direction by the prevailing wind.

He turned, a look of relief flashing across his face as he saw her standing there. 'No, leaving.' In response to her raised brow, he added in a hard voice, 'Ariana. I gave her her marching orders.'

Theo's expression softened as he took her by the shoulders. 'What did he say?' he asked, tipping his head in the direction of her bedroom.

'I'm fine… Theo, Ariana…'

His jaw tightened. 'We will not discuss that woman.'

Beth ignored the instruction. 'We have to, Theo. Did you ask her to leave because of the swimming incident? Because she might not have known; it might have been an innocent mistake.'

'You think the best of people, which is not a bad thing,' he admitted huskily. 'It is one of the things that makes you…' He stopped, his deep voice breaking. 'But with people like Ariana…' He shook his head. 'That is not a good idea, Beth. I blame myself.'

The lash of self-recrimination in his voice as he dragged a hand through his hair made Beth shake her head in protest. 'Is there anything you don't blame yourself for?' she teased.

'This is no joke, Beth. I brought the woman into your life.' There was dark anguish shining in his eyes as he cupped her face between his hands. 'I knew what she was like, what she was capable of,' he confessed between clenched teeth. 'Though I never imagined for one moment that you'd be in danger. You must believe that,' he said urgently.

'Of course I believe you.'

'The fact remains that I exposed you to danger. I used you. If anything had happened to you….' He closed his eyes on the nightmare images in his mind.

'But they didn't, Theo,' Beth said, moved beyond measure by the pain in this strong man's face. Then, knowing she would not be able to shake the jealousy aroused by the stories that had circulated after the brothers' row, she blurted, 'Do you still have feelings for her?'

He looked astonished by the suggestion but not, to her relief, particularly offended by her curiosity. 'Beyond loathing, you mean?'

'You didn't want Andreas to marry her.'

Theo exhaled a long gusty sigh and squared his shoulders. 'Let me tell you a story about Ariana.'

He took her by the hand and led her off the balcony indoors, opening the door to a room that appeared to be a studio. Beth lifted one of the canvases stacked against a wall and caught her breath.

It wasn't just the vivid colours of the seascape that leapt off the canvas but the raw emotion and startling beauty conveyed by the confident bold strokes of the artist.

'This is extraordinary,' she gasped before lifting the one behind it—a different subject this time, a young boy's face. She frowned at the familiarity of the delicate features, then turned with a gasp to Theo. 'Your brother?'

Theo gave a self-conscious shrug. 'As I remember him.'

Her eyes misted. 'You remember him with love.' It shone off the canvas. 'You painted all of these?' Her gesture took in the stacked canvases along the walls. There were at least a dozen—more.

Again, he nodded.

She shook her head in utter astonishment. This man she loved was such a maze of contradictions.

'You're talented, Theo, very talented. Why haven't I seen any of your work on the walls here?' She was sure she would have recognised the distinctive style.

'I paint a little when I am here, but just for myself.' He studied the painting she held before turning it back to the wall and explaining, 'My father did not approve of my artistic *pretensions*.'

'But why?' she exclaimed. It seemed extraordinary to Beth that any parent would not encourage a child who displayed this sort of talent to explore his gift, rather than stifle it. His father should have been proud, not made him guilty of his talent, she thought angrily.

'He considered it a distraction and not,' he admitted with a twisted smile, 'manly.'

A choked little laugh left Beth's lips. 'Your father sounds—'

'He was a man of his generation and he had many good points; he was just not exactly touchy-feely. It was not until after his death that I began to paint a little again. Come,' he added, pulling a dust sheet off a chair and pressed her down into it. 'You want to know about Ariana.'

'Not if you don't want to—'

'Six years ago, I ended our engagement.'

'You ended the engagement!' she echoed. 'But I thought…'

'I ended the engagement. You know that her first marriage ended in divorce?' Beth nodded. 'To cut, as they say, a long story short, I walked in one day and found her in bed with her stepson.'

Beth's jaw dropped.

'My pride was hurt, Elizabeth, not my heart.' He took her hand and placed it on his chest. 'That belongs to you,' he told her thickly.

'Oh, Theo!' she whispered, looking up at him with shining eyes. 'I love you,' she declared huskily.

'There is more to my story. The boy's father was with me at the time. He was the intended audience—Ariana's petty revenge for being deprived of a property she particularly wanted in the divorce settlement. The woman is motivated by greed and revenge. I never loved Ariana. I was idealistic, young and confused lust for love. With you,' he added throatily, 'I have both.'

Beth sighed happily and said, 'Hold that thought.' She added, 'What I don't understand is why you and Andreas fought over Ariana.'

He arched a brow. 'This is news to me.'

Beth shook her head. 'I know it happened; the place was buzzing with your big row.'

'We had a *big row*, as you call it,' he conceded. 'But

not about Ariana, although she was mentioned, but so were you.'

'I was? You weren't fighting over me?'

Theo trailed a finger down her cheek. The loving expression in his eyes made Beth's heart skip a happy beat.

'Would you like it if we were fighting over you?' he teased.

Beth was indignant. 'What a thing to ask—of course I wouldn't...' She stopped, gave a grin and added, 'Well, not exactly...*were you*?'

His grin widened. 'Our conversation that morning left me with the distinct impression you wished it had been Andreas and not me the night before.'

Beth's jaw dropped. 'How could you think that?'

'How?' Theo stared at her incredulously. 'You did say you loved him.'

For years Theo had dismissed Andreas's petty jealousies out of hand. Now, with the situation reversed—and there was nothing approaching petty about the dark emotions he was experiencing—he actually felt a lot more sympathy for his brother.

He had even restrained himself from pointing out such home truths when Andreas had confided that actually he might not be in love with Ariana.

Beth grimaced at the reminder. 'I thought I was,' she admitted. 'But I had no idea then that love needed passion and passion needed love and how rare it is to find the two in one place, or,' she added, lifting a loving hand to his face, 'one person.'

'The point is, I thought the one person was Andreas and I went to discuss the situation with my little brother in a civilised manner.'

Beth rolled her eyes and said, 'Who threw the first punch?'

Theo grinned back. 'Andreas did not take kindly to being told that a man who played footsie with one woman was not ready to marry another.'

'I shouldn't have told you that,' Beth said with a wince.

Theo did not agree. 'You should always tell me everything,' he rasped, adding weight to the suggestion by fitting his lips to hers and kissing her deeply.

'No secrets?' she teased, emerging breathless and blissfully happy from the embrace.

'None.'

She nodded her agreement.

'Things actually did not get really nasty until I mentioned the fact that if he cheated on you ever I would crush him like a bug.'

Beth's eyes were round. 'You actually said that?'

'Not those exact words,' he conceded with a grin. 'I gave you the censored version.'

'Did you make him go to New Zealand?'

'No, it was his idea. I think he was having some doubts about Ariana and he wanted some space to review his options.'

Beth bit her lip and lowered her eyes. Was that what Theo would be doing in a few months' time? She pushed away the intrusive thought—why worry about an unknown future when you could enjoy today?

'I actually think,' he mused, 'that Andreas waited so long to decide he was dumping Ariana because I told him to.'

'I react that way when you tell me to do things.'

'Not always,' he said. 'There have been moments when you seemed *very* eager to please me.'

When he took her hands and pulled her to her feet she came willingly. The wicked gleam in his eyes made her flush, then shiver when he slid his hand up her body, stopping only when he reached her breast.

Her little cry of pain made him drop his hand and look at her with concern. 'You were lying—you are injured.'

'No,' she promised him. 'I didn't lie. It's fine—I'm just a little tender there.'

He watched her lightly touch her breasts and frowned. 'Why would you be?' He stopped, the colour draining from his face as he stared at her. 'You mean you are...'

His eyes dropped to her flat stomach and he swallowed hard.

'No need to panic just yet. I'm not one hundred per cent sure, but it is possible.'

His eyes lifted to her face. 'But you think you are?'

Beth stole a look at his face and was comforted to see that he didn't look too bad, considering the shock she had just delivered. She expelled a gusty sigh, nodded and said, 'I'm sorry.'

He stared at her. 'Why would you be sorry?'

'Well, it's not like you planned for this to happen.'

Theo took her chin in his hand and forced her face up to his. 'I did not plan to fall in love with you either, but it is still the best thing that has ever happened to me.'

The simple statement brought tears to her eyes.

'Some things are meant to be.'

She studied his face warily. 'So you wouldn't mind?'

'Mind?' he echoed. 'I'd be delighted.'

Beth felt the last cloud vanish from her horizon.

'You do realise that a baby with us as parents will no doubt be brilliant and gifted and very *very* beautiful?' he told her, his eyes gleaming as they swept her face. 'And this settles it—why wait? We could get married next week, actually,' he mused, visibly warming to the idea. 'Tomorrow.'

'You want me to marry you?'

He looked amazed by the question. 'Well, that's a given, obviously.'

'Not to me. I thought you wanted an affair, but marriage...? It didn't even cross my mind,' she admitted. 'You're not saying this because of the baby?'

He shook his head. 'I want to commit to you. I want to do that legally and for keeps.'

Beth gave up on trying to blot the tears streaming down her cheeks—there were too many. 'Theo—' her husky voice was shaky '—a woman likes to be asked.'

Without a second thought, he dropped down onto one knee. 'Elizabeth Farley, will you do me the honour of being my wife?'

She pressed a finger to the dimple in her chin, sniffed and pretended to think about it. 'Well, let me see...' She let out a whoop of protest as he leapt to his feet and, with his arms banded around her hips, lifted her high in the air.

'Put me down, you idiot!' she shouted as he whirled her around.

'Not until you say yes.'

'All right, yes, I will marry you.'

A fierce predatory grin spread across his face. 'Right answer,' he said slowly, lowering her but keeping her body very close to his as he did so. When her feet hit the floor, his hand stayed on her bottom.

'Do I get a prize?' she asked huskily.

'You get me.'

'Nice, but do I get a prize?' she teased.

'Actually, now you mention it, I do have. Wait there.' He vanished through a door and returned a moment later carrying something long and cylindrical. 'More a wedding present.'

Frowning her puzzlement, Beth slid the papers from the document case and opened them. She stared at the plans, not really understanding what she was seeing, then she suddenly recognised the shape of— Her startled gaze flew to his face.

'This is my house, though not actually mine any more. I just sold it,' she informed him. The sale had gone through earlier; she had received the agent's text on the journey there.

'I know.'

She shook her head. 'I don't understand.'

'I bought the house for you. The architect who drew up the plans has worked on a lot of period properties, but obviously he will incorporate anything you want. Maybe the nursery could be—'

'You bought my house for me?'

Theo watched with alarm as her lips began to tremble and her luminous eyes filled afresh.

'If you prefer to live somewhere else—'

Beth blinked back the tears misting her vision and, reaching up, she took his face between her hands. 'I would live anywhere with you, Theo,' she declared with a smile that took his breath away, 'but this is probably the loveliest thing that anyone has ever done for me. But when you bought it you didn't know I would be coming.'

Her sweet naivety drew a smile from him. 'Who do you think arranged for you to be here?'

'Your mother asked me. She said that you—'

'My mother said what I asked her to.'

'Then it was a conspiracy.'

'Most definitely,' he agreed. 'And one that worked very well, except for the one fly in the ointment—Ariana.'

'Were there ever any guests? And your mother and Georgios— there was no work crisis? Were you so sure of me?'

'I was sure that I did not want to spend another day without you and did not want to share you with anyone.'

She shook her head. 'You are a very sneaky man.'

'I am the man you need.'

This arrogant assertion was so Theo that it made her smile. The smile was absent as she corrected him. '*Want* and need,' she admitted with a husky throb in her voice.

His eyes darkened as his heated gaze hungrily devoured the face turned up to him. 'I am interested in how much you *need* and *want* me.'

Beth was happy to show him and it turned out to be quite a lot!

MODERN

THE RELUCTANT SURRENDER
by Penny Jordan

Working with Giselle Freeman, it's obvious to Saul Parenti that beneath her arctic façade lies a fiery passion… And with Saul challenging her defences, the only possible outcome is *surrender*!

The Virgin's Choice
by Jennie Lucas

When Xerxes Novros whisks Rose away to his private Greek island, he is determined to give her the wedding night she's been denied… Now the kidnapped virgin bride has a choice… or does she?

Powerful Greek, Housekeeper Wife
by Robyn Donald

Shy Iona Guthrie has had to consign her passionate affair with tycoon Luke Michelakis to memory. But then Luke makes a startling proposition and he knows Iona will meet *all* his requirements…

Snowbound Seduction
by Helen Brooks

Sensible Rachel Ellington doesn't understand why she is being pursued by millionaire businessman Zac Lawson! But when the wintry weather provides the perfect setting for seduction, she knows exactly why she was so nervous…

On sale from 17th September 2010
Don't miss out!

*Available at WHSmith, Tesco, ASDA, Eason
and all good bookshops*

www.millsandboon.co.uk

SHAMEFUL SECRET, SHOTGUN WEDDING
by Sharon Kendrick

Shop assistant Cassie Summers agrees to be international playboy Giancarlo Vellutini's mistress for Christmas… But will an unexpected gift make this temporary arrangement last a lifetime?

SCANDAL: UNCLAIMED LOVE-CHILD
by Melanie Milburne

Billionaire Luca Sabbatini may have ruthlessly cast Bronte from his life, but he hasn't forgotten the sweet ballerina. He's ready to reawaken their lost passion – however, the secret she's hiding will have its repercussions!

HIRED BY HER HUSBAND
by Anne McAllister

When Sophy wakes up and realises her marriage to George Savas is a sham, she never looks back. But when stubborn and proud George wants her help, he soon realises that his need for Sophy runs deep…

A MISTAKE, A PRINCE AND A PREGNANCY
by Maisey Yates

Eternally single Alison Whitman is carrying the *royal heir* of the Prince of Turan! Maximo will seize this surprise chance at fatherhood, but he'll never stand for an illegitimate heir…

On sale from 1st October 2010
Don't miss out!

Available at WHSmith, Tesco, ASDA, Eason and all good bookshops

www.millsandboon.co.uk

2 FREE BOOKS
AND A SURPRISE GIFT

We would like to take this opportunity to thank you for reading this Mills & Boon® book by offering you the chance to take TWO more specially selected books from the Modern™ series absolutely FREE! We're also making this offer to introduce you to the benefits of the Mills & Boon® Book Club™—

- **FREE home delivery**
- **FREE gifts and competitions**
- **FREE monthly Newsletter**
- **Exclusive Mills & Boon Book Club offers**
- **Books available before they're in the shops**

Accepting these FREE books and gift places you under no obligation to buy, you may cancel at any time, even after receiving your free books. Simply complete your details below and return the entire page to the address below. You don't even need a stamp!

YES Please send me 2 free Modern books and a surprise gift. I understand that unless you hear from me, I will receive 4 superb new books every month for just £3.19 each, postage and packing free. I am under no obligation to purchase any books and may cancel my subscription at any time. The free books and gift will be mine to keep in any case.

Ms/Mrs/Miss/Mr _____ Initials _____

Surname _____

Address _____

_____

_____ Postcode _____

E-mail _____

Send this whole page to: Mills & Boon Book Club, Free Book Offer, FREEPOST NAT 10298, Richmond, TW9 1BR

Offer valid in UK only and is not available to current Mills & Boon Book Club subscribers to this series. Overseas and Eire please write for details.. We reserve the right to refuse an application and applicants must be aged 18 years or over. Only one application per household. Terms and prices subject to change without notice. Offer expires 30th November 2010. As a result of this application, you may receive offers from Harlequin Mills & Boon and other carefully selected companies. If you would prefer not to share in this opportunity please write to The Data Manager, PO Box 676, Richmond, TW9 1WU.

Mills & Boon® is a registered trademark owned by Harlequin Mills & Boon Limited.
Modern™ is being used as a trademark. The Mills & Boon® Book Club™ is being used as a trademark.